To my sister-in-law, Danielle Cast,
also known as my French expert.

ACKNOWLEDGMENTS

Thanks to Kim Doner, for the incredible art and for her friendship. XXXOOO

A big thank-you to my sister-in-law, for saving me from my pathetic French. Any mistakes that end up in the text are mine and mine alone (sorry to my French readers!).

Christine—I heart you totally.

As always, I want to thank my St. Martin's family, for being a Dream Team, as well as my agent and friend, Meredith Bernstein, without whom the House of Night wouldn't exist

CHAPTER ONE

February 1788, France

"*Elle est morte!*"

Lenobia's world exploded with the sound of a scream and three small words.

"She is dead?" Jeanne, the scullery maid working beside her, paused in her kneading of the plump, fragrant bread dough.

"*Oui*, may the Holy Mother have mercy on Cecile's soul."

Lenobia looked up to see her mother standing in the arched doorway to the kitchen. Her pretty face was unusually pale and her hand clutched the worn rosary beads that were always looped around her neck.

Lenobia shook her head in disbelief. "But just days ago she was laughing and singing. I heard her. I saw her!"

"She was beautiful, but never strong, that poor girl," Jeanne said, shaking her head sadly. "Always so pale. Half of the château caught that same ague, my sister and brother included. They recovered easily."

"Death, he strikes quickly and terribly," Lenobia's

mother said. "Lord or servant, he eventually comes for each of us."

Forever after, the yeasty scent of fresh bread would remind Lenobia of death and sicken her stomach.

Jeanne shuddered and crossed herself with a flour-whitened hand, leaving a crescent-shaped spot in the middle of her forehead. "May the Mother protect us."

Automatically, Lenobia genuflected, though her eyes never left her mother's face.

"Come with me, Lenobia. I need your help more than Jeanne does."

Lenobia would never forget the feeling of dread that engulfed her with her mother's words.

"But there will be guests—mourners—we must have bread," Lenobia stammered. Her mother's gray eyes, so like her own, turned to storm clouds. "That was not a request," she said, switching smoothly from French to English.

"When your *mère* speaks in the barbaric English, you know she must be obeyed." Jeanne shrugged her round shoulders and got back to her dough kneading.

Lenobia wiped her hands on a linen towel and forced herself to hurry to her mother. Elizabeth Whitehall nodded at her daughter and then turned, motioning for Lenobia to follow her.

They made their way quickly through the wide, graceful halls of the Château de Navarre. There were nobles who had more money than the Baron of Bouillon—he was not one of King Louis's confidants or courtiers, but he did have a family that could be traced back hundreds of years, and a country estate that was the envy of many lords who were richer, though not as well-bred.

Today the château's halls were hushed and the curved, mullioned windows that usually allowed plentiful sunlight to spill against the clean marble floors were already being draped with heavy black velvet by a legion of silent servant girls. Lenobia thought that the house itself seemed muffled with grief and shock.

Then Lenobia realized they were hurrying away from the central part of the manor and toward one of the rear exits that would empty out near the stables.

"Maman, où allons-nous?"

"In English! You know I loathe the sound of French," her mother snapped.

Lenobia suppressed a sigh of irritation and switched to her mother's birth language. "Where are you going?"

Her mother glanced around them, then grabbed her daughter's hand and, in a low, tight voice said, "You must trust me and do exactly as I say."

"Of-of course I trust you, Mother," Lenobia said, frightened by the wild look in her mother's eyes.

Elizabeth's expression softened and she touched her daughter's cheek. "You are a good girl. You always have been. Your circumstances are my fault, my sin alone."

Lenobia began to shake her head. "No, it wasn't your sin! The Baron takes whomever he wants as a mistress. You were too beautiful not to catch his eye. That was not your fault."

Elizabeth smiled, which allowed some of her past loveliness to surface. "Ah, but I was not beautiful enough to keep his eye, and because I was only the daughter of an English farmer, the Baron cast me aside, though I suppose I must eternally be grateful he found a place for me, and for you, in his household."

Lenobia felt the old bitterness burn within her. "He took you from England—stole you from your family. And I am his daughter. He should find a place for me, and for my mother."

"You are his bastard daughter," Elizabeth corrected her. "And only one of many—though by far the prettiest. As pretty even as his legitimate daughter, the poor, dead Cecile."

Lenobia looked away from her mother. It was an uncomfortable truth that she and her half sister did look very much alike, enough alike to have caused rumors and whispers as both girls began to bloom into young women. Over the past two years Lenobia had learned it was best to avoid her sister and the rest of the Baron's family, who all seemed to detest the very sight of her. She had found it easier to escape to the stables—somewhere Cecile, the Baroness, and her three brothers rarely went. The thought crossed her mind that her life would either be much easier now that the sister who looked so much like her—but who would not acknowledge her—was dead, or the dark looks and the sharp words from the Baroness and her boys would get even worse.

"I am sorry Cecile is dead," Lenobia said aloud, trying to reason through the jumble of her thoughts.

"I would not wish ill on the child, but if she was fated to die, I am grateful that it happened now, at this moment." Elizabeth took her daughter's chin and forced her to meet her gaze. "Cecile's death will mean life for you."

"Life? For me? But I already have a life."

"Yes, the life of a bastard servant in a household that despises the fact that their lord scatters his seed aimlessly and then enjoys flaunting the fruits of his transgressions as if that proves his manhood over and over again. That is not the life I wish for my only child."

"But, I do not under—"

"Come, and you will understand," her mother interrupted, taking her hand again and pulling her along the hallway until they came to a small room near one of the rear doors of the château. Elizabeth opened the door and led Lenobia into the poorly lit room. She moved purposefully to a large basket like those used to carry the linens to wash. There was, indeed, a sheet draped over the top of it. Her mother pulled it away to expose a gown that shimmered with blue and ivory and gray, even in the dim light.

Lenobia stared as her mother began lifting the gown and the expensive undergarments from the basket, shaking them out, smoothing their wrinkles, brushing off the delicate velvet slippers. She glanced at her daughter. "You must hurry. If we are to be successful, we have very little time."

"Mother? I—"

"You are going to put on these clothes, and with them you will also put on the identity of another. Today you will become Cecile Marson de La Tour d'Auvergne, the legitimate daughter of the Baron of Bouillon."

Lenobia wondered if her mother had gone utterly mad. "Mother, everyone knows Cecile is dead."

"No, my child. Everyone at the Château de Navarre knows she is dead. No one on the coach that will be here within the hour to transport Cecile to the port of Le Havre, or on the ship awaiting her there, knows she is dead. Nor will they, because Cecile is going to meet that coach and take that ship to the New World, the new husband, and the new life that awaits her in New Orleans as a legitimate daughter of a French baron."

"I cannot!"

Her mother dropped the gown and grasped both of her daughter's hands, squeezing them so hard Lenobia would have flinched had she not been so shocked. "You must! Do you know what awaits you here? You are almost sixteen. You have been fully a woman for two summers. You hide in the stables—you hide in the kitchen—but you cannot hide forever. I saw how the Marquis looked at you last month, and then again last week." Her mother shook her head, and Lenobia was shocked to realize she was fighting back tears as she continued to speak. "You and I have not spoken of it, but you must know that the true reason we have not attended Mass at Évreux these past weeks is not because my duties have overtired me."

"I wondered . . . but I did not want to know!" Lenobia pressed her trembling lips together, afraid of what else she might say.

"You must face the truth."

Lenobia drew a deep breath, yet still a shudder of fear moved through her body. "The Bishop of Évreux—I could almost feel the heat of his eyes when he stared at me."

"I have heard he does much more than stare at young girls," her mother said. "There is something unholy about that man—something more than the sin of his corporeal desires. Lenobia, Daughter, I cannot protect you from him or any other man because the Baron will not protect you. Becoming someone else and escaping the life sentence that it means to be a bastard is your only answer."

Lenobia gripped her mother's hands as if they were a lifeline and stared into the eyes so much like her own. *My mother is right. I know she is right.* "I have to be brave enough to do this." Lenobia spoke her thought aloud.

"You are brave enough to do this. You have the blood of courageous Englishmen pounding through your veins. Remember that, and it will strengthen you."

"I will remember."

"Very well, then." Her mother nodded resolutely. "Take those servant's rags off and we will dress you anew." She squeezed her daughter's hands before releasing them and turning back to the pile of shimmering cloth.

When Lenobia's trembling hands faltered, her mother's took over, swiftly divesting her of the simple but familiar clothing. Elizabeth didn't even leave Lenobia her home-spun shift, and for a dizzying moment it seemed she was even shedding her old skin for new. She didn't pause until her daughter was totally naked. Then, in complete silence, Elizabeth dressed Lenobia carefully, layer upon layer: shift, pockets, panniers, under petticoat, over petticoat, stays, stomacher, and the lovely silk robe *à la polonaise*. It was only after she had helped her on with the slippers, fussed with her hair, and then swirled a fur-trimmed, hooded pelisse around her shoulders that she finally stepped back, curtseyed deeply, and said, *"Bonjour, Mademoiselle Cecile, votre carrosse attend."*

"Maman, no! This plan—I understand why you must send me away, but how can you bear it?" Lenobia pressed her hand over her mouth, trying to silence the sob that was building there.

Elizabeth Whitehall simply rose, took her daughter's shoulders, and said, "I can bear it because of the great love I bear for you." Slowly, she turned Lenobia so that she could see her reflection in the large, cracked mirror that rested on the floor behind them, waiting to be replaced.

"Look, child."

Lenobia gasped and reached toward the reflection, too startled to do anything except stare.

"Except for your eyes and the lightness of your hair, you are the image of her. Know it. Believe it. Become her."

Lenobia's gaze went from the mirror to her mother. "No! I cannot be her. God rest her soul, but Cecile was not a kind girl. Mother, you know she cursed me every time she saw me, even though we share the same blood. Please, Maman, do not make me do this. Do not make me become her."

Elizabeth touched her daughter's cheek. "My sweet, strong girl. You could never become like Cecile, and I would never ask it of you. Take only her name. Inside, in here." Her touch went from Lenobia's face to the spot on her breast under which her heart beat tremulously. "In here you will always be Lenobia Whitehall. Know that. Believe that. And in doing so you will become more than her."

Lenobia swallowed the dryness in her throat and the terrible pounding of her heart. "I hear you. I believe you. I will take on her name but not become her."

"Good. It is settled then." Her mother reached behind the laundry basket and lifted a small, box-shaped case. "Here, take this. The rest of her trunks were sent to the port days ago."

"La casquette de Cecile." Lenobia took it hesitantly.

"Do not use the vulgar French word for it. They make it sound like a casket. It is a travel case. That is all. It is meant as the beginning of a new life—not the ending of an old one."

"It has her jewelry in it. I heard Nicole and Anne talking." The other servants had gossiped incessantly about how the Baron had ignored Cecile for sixteen years, but now that she was being sent away he lavished jewelry and attention on her as the Baroness wept about losing her only daughter. "Why did the Baron agree to send Cecile to the New World?"

Her mother snorted in disdain. "His latest mistress, that opera singer, has almost bankrupted him. The King is paying handsomely for titled, virtuous daughters willing to marry the nobility of New Orleans."

"The Baron sold his daughter?"

"He did. His excess has purchased you a new life. Now, let us go so that you might claim it." Her mother cracked the door and peered into the hallway. She turned back to Lenobia. "No one is about. Put your hood over your hair. Follow me. Quickly."

"But the coach will be stopped by the liverymen. The drivers will be told about Cecile."

"Yes, if the coach was allowed to enter the estate they would be told. That is why we shall meet it outside the grand gates. You will board it there."

There was no time to argue with her mother. It was almost mid-morning, and there should have been servants and tradesmen and visitors coming and going from the busy estate. But today there was a pall over everything. Even the sun's face was veiled as mist and low, murky clouds swirled over the château.

She was certain they would be stopped, would be found out, but sooner than it seemed possible the huge iron gate loomed out of the mist. Her mother opened the smaller walkway exit, and they hurried into the road.

"You will tell the coach driver that there is an ague at the château, so the Baron sent you out so that no one would be contaminated. Remember, you are the daughter of nobility. Expect to be obeyed."

"Yes, Mother."

"Good. You have always seemed older than your years, and now I understand why. You cannot be a child any longer, my beautiful, brave daughter. You must become a woman."

"But, Maman, I—" Lenobia began, but her mother's words silenced her.

"Listen to me and know that I am telling you the truth. I believe in you. I believe in your strength, Lenobia. I also believe in your goodness." Her mother paused and then slowly took the old rosary beads from around her neck and lifted them, placing them over her daughter's head, and tucking them under the lace stomacher so that they were pressed against her skin, invisible to everyone. "Take these. Remember that I believe in you, and know that even though we must be apart, I will always be part of you."

It was only then that the true realization hit Lenobia. She would never see her mother again.

"No." Her voice sounded strange, too high, too fast, and she was having trouble catching her breath. "Maman! You must come with me!"

Elizabeth Whitehall took her daughter in her arms. "I cannot. The *fille du roi* are not allowed servants. There is little room on the ship." She hugged Lenobia tightly, speaking quickly as, in the distance, the sound of a coach echoed through the mist. "I know that I have been hard on you, but that was only because you had to grow brave and strong. I have always loved you, Lenobia. You are the best, the finest thing in my life. I will think of you and miss you every day, for as long as I live."

"No, Maman," Lenobia sobbed. "I cannot say good-bye to you. I cannot do this."

"You will do this for me. You will live the life I could not give you. Be brave, my beautiful child. Remember who you are."

"How do I remember who I am if I am pretending to be someone else?" Lenobia cried. Elizabeth stepped back and gently wiped the wetness from her daughter's cheeks. "You will remember here." Once more, her mother pressed the palm of her hand against Lenobia's chest over her heart. "You shall stay true to me, and to yourself, here. In your heart you will always know, always remember. As in mine, I will always know, always remember you."

Then the coach burst into the road beside them, causing mother and daughter to stumble back out of the way.

"Whoa!" The driver of the coach pulled his team up and shouted at Lenobia and her mother. "What are you doing there, you women? Do you want to be killed?"

"You will not speak to the Mademoiselle Cecile Marson de La Tour d'Auvergne in such a voice!" her mother yelled at the coachman. His gaze skittered to Lenobia, who brushed the tears from her cheeks with the back of her hand, lifted her chin, and glared at the driver.

"Mademoiselle d'Auvergne? But why are you out here?"

"There is a sickness at the château. My father, the Baron, has kept me separate from it so that I am not contagious." Lenobia's hand went to her chest and she pressed against the lacy fabric there so that her mother's rosary beads bit into her skin, grounding her, giving her strength. But still she could not help reaching out and clinging to her mother's hand for security.

"Are you daft, man? Do you not see the mademoiselle has waited here for you for far too long already? Help her inside the coach and out of this horrid dampness before she does fall ill," her mother snapped at the servant.

The driver scrambled down immediately, opening the door to the coach and offering his hand.

Lenobia felt as if all of the air had been knocked from her body. She looked wildly at her mother.

Tears were washing down her mother's face, but she simply curtseyed deeply and said, "*Bon voyage* to you, child."

Lenobia ignored the gaping coachman and pulled her mother up, hugging her so tightly the rosary beads dug painfully into her skin. "Tell my mother I love her and will remember her and miss her every day of my life," she said in a shaky voice.

"And my prayer, to the Holy Mother of us all, is that she let this sin be attributed to me. Let this curse be on my head, not yours," Elizabeth whispered against her daughter's cheek.

Then she broke Lenobia's embrace, curtseyed again, and turned away, walking with no hesitation back the way they'd come.

"Mademoiselle d'Auvergne?" Lenobia looked at the coachman. "Shall I take the *casquette* for you?"

"No," she said woodenly, surprised that her voice still worked. "I'll keep my *casquette* with me." He gave her an odd look but held out his hand for her. She saw her hand being placed in his, and her legs carried her up and into the coach. He bowed briefly and then clambered back to his position as driver. As the coach lurched forward, Lenobia turned to look back at the gates of the Château de Navarre and saw her mother collapsed to the ground, weeping with both hands covering her mouth to stifle her wails of grief.

Hand pressed against the expensive glass of the carriage window, Lenobia sobbed, watching her mother and her world fade into mist and memory.

CHAPTER TWO

With a swirl of skirts and throaty, low laughter, Laetitia disappeared around a marble wall carved with images of saints, leaving only the scent of her perfume and the remnants of unsatisfied desire in her wake.

Charles cursed, *"Ah, ventrebleu!"* and adjusted his velvet robes.

"Father?" the acolyte repeated, calling down the inner hallway that ran behind the chancel of the cathedral. "Did you hear me? It is the Archbishop! He is here and asking for you."

"I heard you!" Father Charles glared at the boy. As the priest approached him, he lifted his hand and made a shooing motion. Charles noted that the child flinched like a skittish colt, which made the priest smile.

Charles's smile was not a pleasant thing to behold, and the boy backed quickly down the steps that led up to the chancel, putting more space between the two of them.

"Where is de Juigne?" Charles asked.

"Not far from here, just inside the main entrance to the cathedral, Father."

"I trust he has not been waiting long?"

"Not too long, Father. But you were, uh—" The boy broke off, his face filled with consternation.

"I was deep in prayer, and you did not wish to disturb me," Charles finished for him, staring hard at the boy.

"Y-yes, Father."

The boy was unable to look away from him. He'd begun to sweat, and his face had turned an alarming shade of pink. Charles couldn't tell if the child was going to cry or explode. Either would have amused the priest.

"Ah, but we have no time for amusement," he mused aloud, breaking his gaze with the boy and walking quickly past him. "We have an unexpected guest." Enjoying the fact that the boy flattened himself against the screening wall so that his priestly robes didn't so much as brush his skin, Charles felt his mood lighten. He shouldn't allow small things to distress him. He would simply call for Laetitia as soon as he could free himself of the Archbishop, and they would resume where they'd left off—which would put her willing and bent before him.

Charles was thinking of Laetitia's shapely bare bottom when he greeted the old priest. "It is a great pleasure to see you, Father Antoine. I am honored to welcome you to the Cathédrale Notre Dame d'Évreux," Charles de Beaumont, Bishop of Évreux, lied smoothly.

"*Merci beaucoup,* Father Charles." The archbishop of Paris, Antoine le Clerc de Juigne, kissed him chastely on one cheek and then the other.

Charles thought the old fool's lips felt dry and dead.

"To what do my cathedral and I owe the pleasure of your visit?"

"Your cathedral, Father? Surely it is more accurate to say that this is God's house."

Charles's anger began to build. Automatically, his long fingers began to stroke the huge ruby cross that always hung from a thick chain around his throat. The flames of the lit votive candles at the feet of the nearby statue of the beheaded Saint Denis fluttered spasmodically.

"To say this is my cathedral is simply a term of endearment and not one of possession," Charles said. "Shall we retire to my offices to share wine and break bread?"

"Indeed, my journey was long, and though in February I should be thankful it is rain and not snow falling from the gray skies, the damp weather is tiring."

"Have the wine and a decent meal brought immediately to my offices." Charles motioned impatiently to one of the nearby acolytes, who jumped nervously before scurrying away to do his bidding. When Charles's gaze returned to the older priest, he saw that de Juigne was studying the retreating acolyte with an expression that was his first warning that something was amiss with this unannounced visit. "Come, Antoine, you do look weary. My offices are warm and welcoming. You will be comfortable there." Charles led the old priest away from the nave, across the cathedral, through the pleasant little garden, and to the opulent offices that adjoined his spacious private chambers. All the while the archbishop gazed around them, silent and contemplative.

It wasn't until they were finally settled in front of Charles's marble fireplace, a goblet of excellent red wine in his hand and a sumptuous repast placed before him, that de Juigne deigned to speak.

"The climate of the world is changing, Father Charles."

Charles raised his brows and wondered if the old man was as daft as he appeared. He'd traveled all the way from Paris to talk of the weather? "Indeed, it seems this winter is warmer and wetter than any in my memory," Charles said, wishing this useless conversation to be over soon.

Antoine le Clerc de Juigne's blue eyes, which had appeared watery and unfocused just seconds before, sharpened. His gaze skewered Charles. "Idiot! Why would I be speaking of the weather? It is the climate of the people that concerns me."

"Ah, of course." For the moment, Charles was too surprised by the sharpness in the old man's voice even to feel anger. "The people."

"There is talk of a revolution."

"There is always talk of a revolution," Charles said, choosing a succulent piece of pork to go with the smooth goat cheese he'd sliced for his bread.

"It is more than simple talk," said the old priest.

"Perhaps," Charles said through a full mouth.

"The world changes around us. We draw near a new century, though I will pass into Grace before it arrives and younger men, men like yourself, will be left to lead the church through the tumult that approaches."

Charles fervently wished the old priest had expired before he'd made this visit, but he hid his feelings, chewed, and nodded sagely, saying only, "I will pray that I am worthy of such a weighty responsibility."

"I am pleased that you are in agreement about the need to take responsibility for your actions," said de Juigne.

Charles narrowed his eyes. "My actions? We were speaking of the people and the change within them."

"Yes, and that is why your actions have come to the attention of His Holiness."

Charles's mouth suddenly went dry and he had to gulp wine to swallow. He tried to speak, but de Juigne continued, not allowing him to talk.

"In times of upheaval, especially as the tide of popular attitude sways toward bourgeois beliefs, it has become increasingly important that the church does not drown in the wake of change." The priest paused to sip delicately at his wine.

"Forgive me, Father. I am at a loss to understand you."

"Oh, I doubt that very much. You could not believe your behavior would be ignored forever. You weaken the church, and that cannot be ignored."

"My behavior? Weaken the church?" Charles was too astounded to be truly angry. He swept a well-manicured hand around them. "Does my church appear weakened to you? I am loved by my parishioners. They show their devotion by tithing with the generosity that fills this table."

"You are feared by your parishioners. They fill your table and your coffers because they are more afraid of the fire of your rage than the burning of their empty stomachs."

Charles's own stomach lurched. *How could the old bastard know? And if he knows, does that mean the Pope does as well?* Charles forced himself to remain calm. He even managed a dry chuckle. "Absurd! If it is fires they fear, it is brought on by the weight of their own sins and the possibility of eternal damnation. So they give generously to me to alleviate those fears, and I duly absolve them."

The Archbishop continued as if Charles had never spoken. "You should have kept to the whores. No one notices what happens to them. Isabelle Varlot was the daughter of a marquis."

Charles's stomach continued to churn. "That girl was the victim of a horrible accident. She passed too close to a torch. A spark lit her dress afire. She burned before anyone could save her."

"She burned after spurning your advances."

"That is ridiculous! I did not—"

"You should also have kept your cruelty in check," the Archbishop interrupted. "Too many of the novices come from noble families. There has been talk."

"Talk!" Charles sputtered.

"Yes, talk supported by the scars of burns. Jean du Bellay returned to his father's barony minus the robes of a priest and instead carrying scars that will disfigure him for the rest of his life."

"It is a shame his faith was not as great as his clumsiness. He almost burned my stables to the ground. It has naught to do with me that after an injury of his own causing he renounced his charge to our priesthood and retreated home to the wealth of his family."

"Jean tells a very different story. He says he confronted you about your cruel treatment of his fellow novices and your anger was so great that you set him, and the stables around him, afire."

Charles felt the rage begin to burn within him, and as he spoke, the flames of the candles in their ornate silver holders that sat at either end of the dining table flickered wildly, growing brighter with each word. "You will not come into my church and make accusations against me."

The old priest's eyes widened as he stared at the growing flames. "It is true what they are saying about you. I did not believe it until now." But instead of retreating or reacting in fear, as Charles had come to expect, de Juigne reached into his robes and pulled out a folded parchment, holding it before him like a warrior's shield.

Charles stroked the ruby cross that sat hot and heavy on his chest. He had actually begun to move his other hand—to flick his fingers toward the nearest candle flame, which writhed brighter and brighter, as if beckoning his touch—but the thick leaden seal on the parchment sent ice through his veins.

"A papal bull!" Charles felt his breath leave him with his words, as if the seal had, indeed, been a shield that had been hurled against his body.

"Yes, His Holiness sent me. His Holiness knows I am

here and, as you may read for yourself, if I or any in my party meet with an unfortunate fiery accident, his mercy will turn to retribution and his vengeance against you will be swift. Had you not been so distracted with defiling the chancel you would have noticed my escort was not made up of priests. The Pope sent his own personal guard with me."

With hands that trembled, Charles took the bull and broke the seal. As he read, the Archbishop's voice filled the chamber around him as if narrating the younger priest's doom.

"You have been watched closely for almost one year. Reports have been made to His Holiness, who has come to the decision that your predilection for fire may not be the manifestation of demonic influence, as many of us believe. His Holiness is willing to give you an opportunity to use your unusual affinity in service of the church by protecting those who are most vulnerable. And nowhere is the church more vulnerable than in New France."

Charles came to the end of the bull and looked up at the Archbishop. "The Pope is sending me to New Orleans."

"He is."

"I will not go. I will not leave my cathedral."

"That is your decision to make, Father Charles. But know that if you choose not to obey, His Holiness has commanded that you be seized by his guards, excommunicated, found guilty of sorcery, and then we shall all see if your love of fire is as great when you are bound to a stake and set ablaze yourself."

"Then I have no choice at all."

The Archbishop shrugged and then stood. "It is more of a choice than I advised you be given."

"When do I leave?"

"You must leave here immediately. It is a two-day carriage ride to Le Havre. In three days the *Minerva* sets sail. His Holiness charges that your protection of the Catholic Church begins the moment you step upon the soil of the New World, where you will take up the seat of Bishop of the Cathedral Saint Louis." Antoine's smile was disdainful. "You will not find New Orleans as generous as Évreux, but you may find that the parishioners in the New World are more forgiving of your, shall we say, eccentricities." The Archbishop began to shuffle toward the door, but he paused and looked back at Charles. "What are you? Tell me truly and I will say nothing to His Holiness."

"I am a humble servant of the church. Anything else has been exaggerated by the jealousy and superstition of others."

The Archbishop shook his head and said no more before leaving the room. As the door closed, Charles fisted both of his hands and smashed them into the table, causing the cutlery and plates to tremble and the flames of the candles to writhe and spill wax down their sides as if they wept with pain.

For the two-day journey from the Château de Navarre to the port of Le Havre, mist and rain wrapped Lenobia's carriage in a veil of gray that was so thick and impenetrable, it seemed to Lenobia that she had been carried from the world she knew and the mother she loved to an unending purgatory. She spoke to no one during the day. The coach paused briefly only for her to attend to the most basic of bodily functions, and then they continued until dark. Each of the two nights, the driver stopped at lovely roadside inns where the madams of the establishments would take charge of Cecile Marson de La Tour d'Auvergne, clucking about her being so young and unchaperoned and, almost beyond her hearing, gossip with the serving girls about how *atroce* and *effrayant* it must be to be on her way to marry a faceless stranger in another world.

"Terrible . . . frightening . . ." Lenobia would repeat. Then she'd hold her mother's rosary beads and pray, "Hail Mary, full of grace, the Lord is with thee, blessed art thou among women . . ." over and over again, just as her mother had for as long as she could remember, until the sounds of the servants' whispering were drowned out by the memory of her mother's voice.

On the third morning they arrived in the port city of Le Havre and, for a fleeting moment, the rain stopped and the mist parted. The scent of fish and the sea permeated everything. When the driver finally stopped and Lenobia stepped from the carriage down to the dock, a brisk, cool breeze chased away the last of the clouds and the sun beamed as if in welcome, flashing on a lavishly painted frigate that bobbed restlessly at anchor nearby in the bay.

Lenobia stared at the ship in awe. All across the top of the hull was a band of blue on which intricate gold filigree was painted that reminded her of flowers and ivy. She could see orange and black and yellow decorating other parts of the hull, as well as the deck. And facing her was the figurehead of a goddess, arms outstretched, gown flowing fiercely in carved and captured wind. She was helmeted as if for war. Lenobia had no idea why, but the sight of the goddess had her breath catching and her heart fluttering.

"*Mademoiselle d'Auvergne? Mademoiselle? Excusez-moi, êtes vous Cecile Marson de La Tour d'Auvergne?*"

The flapping of the nun's brown habit caught Lenobia's attention before her words were truly understandable. *Am I Cecile?* With a jolt Lenobia realized that the Sister had been calling to her from across the dock, and in getting no response, the nun had broken from a group of richly dressed young women and approached her, concern clear in her expression as well as her voice.

"It—it is beautiful!" Lenobia blurted the first thought that fully formed in her mind.

The nun smiled. "It is, indeed. And if you are Cecile Marson de La Tour d'Auvergne you will be pleased to know that it is more than just beautiful. It is the means by which you will embark upon an entirely new life."

Lenobia drew a deep breath, pressed her hand to her breast so that she could feel the pressure of her mother's rosary beads, and said, "Yes, I am Cecile Marson de La Tour d'Auvergne."

"Oh, I am so glad! I am Sister Marie Madeleine Hachard,

and you are the last of the mademoiselles. Now that you are here we can board." The nun's brown eyes were kind. "Is it not a lovely omen that you brought the sun with your arrival?"

"I hope so, Sister Marie Madeleine," Lenobia said, and then had to walk quickly to catch up with the nun as she hurried, with a flutter of her robes, back to the waiting, staring girls.

"It is Mademoiselle d'Auvergne, and we are now all arrived." The nun motioned imperiously to several dock-hands who were standing about doing nothing more than sneaking curious looks at the group of girls. "*Allons-y!* Take us to the *Minerva,* and be careful and quick about it. Commodore Cornwallis is eager to sail with the tide." As the men were scrambling to do her bidding and get a row-boat ready to transport them to the ship, the nun turned back to the girls. With a sweep of her hand she said, "Mademoiselles, let us step into the future!"

Lenobia joined the group, quickly scanning the girls' faces, holding her breath and hoping that none of them would be familiar to her. She breathed a long, shaky sigh of relief when all she recognized was the similarity of their fearful expressions. Even so, she purposefully remained on the outskirts of the women, focusing her gaze and her attention on the ship and the rowboat that would take them to it.

"*Bonjour, Cecile.*" A girl who looked as if she could not be older than thirteen spoke to Lenobia with a soft, shy voice. "*Je m'appelle Simonette LaVigne.*"

"*Bonjour,*" Lenobia said, trying to smile.

The girl moved closer to her. "Are you very, very afraid?"

Lenobia studied her. She was certainly beautiful, with long, dark hair curling over her shoulders and a smooth, guileless face the color of new cream, her complexion marred only by two bright pink spots on her cheeks. She was terrified, Lenobia realized.

Lenobia glanced at the rest of the girls in the group, this time really seeing them. They were all attractive, well dressed, and about her age. They were also wide-eyed and trembling. A few of them were weeping softly. One of the little blondes was shaking her head over and over and clutching a diamond-encrusted crucifix that hung from her neck on a thick gold chain. *They are all afraid,* Lenobia thought.

She smiled at Simonette, and this time actually managed more than a grimace. "No, I am not afraid," Lenobia heard herself say in a voice that sounded much stronger than she felt. "I think the ship is beautiful."

"B-but I c-cannot swim!" stammered the trembling little blonde.

Swim? I am worried about being discovered as an impostor, never seeing my mother again, and facing life in a strange, foreign land. How could she be worried about swimming? The burst of laughter that escaped Lenobia drew the attention of all the girls, as well as Sister Marie Madeleine.

"Do you laugh at me, mademoiselle?" the girl asked her.

Lenobia cleared her throat and said, "No, of course not. I was only thinking how funny we would all look trying to swim to the New World. We would be like floating flowers." She laughed again, this time less hysterically. "But is it not better that we have this magnificent ship to swim us there, instead?"

"What is this talk of swimming?" said Sister Marie Madeleine. "None of us need know how to swim. Mademoiselle Cecile was right to laugh at such a thought." The nun walked to the edge of the dock, where the sailors were waiting impatiently for the girls to begin boarding. "Now, come along. We need to get settled into our quarters so the *Minerva* can get under way." Without so much as a backward glance, Sister Marie Madeleine took the hand of the nearest sailor and stepped awkwardly but enthusiastically into the bobbing rowboat. She had taken a seat and was rearranging her voluminous brown habit before she noticed none of the girls had followed her.

Lenobia noted that several of the mademoiselles had taken steps backward, and tears seemed to be spreading like a pestilence through the group.

This isn't as terrifying as leaving my mother, Lenobia told herself firmly. *Nor is it as frightening as being the bastard daughter of an uncaring baron.* With no more hesitation, Lenobia strode to the edge of the dock. She held out her hand, as if she were accustomed to servants automatically being there to help her, and before she had time to rethink her boldness, she was in the little boat taking a seat on the bench beside Sister Marie Madeleine. The nun reached over and squeezed her hand briefly but firmly.

"That was well done," said the Sister.

Lenobia lifted her chin and met Simonette's gaze. "Come on, little flower! You have nothing to fear."

"Oui!" Simonette said, picking up her skirts and hurrying forward to take the sailor's offered hand. "If you can do it, I can do it."

And that broke the dam of resistance. Soon all of the girls were being handed into the boat. Tears turned to smiles as the confidence of the group built and their terror evaporated, leaving relieved sighs and even some hesitant laughter.

Lenobia wasn't sure when her own smile changed from something inauthentic that she'd forced to honest pleasure, but as the last girl clambered aboard she realized the tightness in her chest had eased, as if the ache in her heart might actually become bearable.

The sailors had rowed them almost all the way to the ship, and Simonette had been chattering about how even though she was almost sixteen years old, she had never before seen the ocean and perhaps she was just a little bit excited, when a gilded carriage pulled up and a tall, purple-robed man exited. He walked to the edge of the dock and glared from the group of girls to the waiting ship. Everything about him—from his stance to the dark look on his face—appeared angry, aggressive, and familiar. Sickeningly familiar . . .

Lenobia was staring at him with a growing feeling of disbelief and dismay. *No, please, let it not be him!*

"His face frightens me." Simonette spoke softly. She, too, was staring at the man on the distant dock.

Sister Marie Madeleine patted her hand reassuringly and responded. "I was notified just this morning that the lovely Cathedral of Saint Louis will be gaining a new bishop. That must be him." The nun smiled kindly at Simonette. "There is no reason for you to be frightened. It is a blessing to have the good bishop traveling with us to New Orleans."

"Do you know which parish he is from?" Lenobia asked, even though she knew the answer before the nun confirmed her dread.

"Why, yes, Cecile. He is Charles de Beaumont, the Bishop of Évreux. But do you not recognize him? I believe Évreux is quite near your home, is it not?"

Feeling as if she were going to be violently ill, Lenobia said, "Yes, Sister. Yes, it is."

CHAPTER THREE

As soon as Lenobia boarded the *Minerva,* she pulled the thick hood of her fur-lined cloak over her head. Forcing herself to ignore the distractions of the brightly painted deck and the bustling energy of everything from crates of flour, bags of salt, and barrels of cured meat, to horses being loaded, Lenobia ducked her chin and tried to disappear. *Horses! There are horses coming with us, too?* She wanted to stare around her and take it all in, but the rowboat had already begun its return trip to the docks, where it would be picking up their fellow traveler, the Bishop of Évreux. *I must get below. I must not let the Bishop see me. Most of all, I must be brave . . . be brave . . . be brave . . .*

"Cecile? Are you well?" Simonette was peering up into her hooded face, sounding so concerned that she drew Sister Marie Madeleine's attention.

"Mademoiselle Cecile, is—"

"I am feeling a little ill, Sister," Lenobia interrupted, trying to speak softly and not call any more attention to herself.

"Aye! 'Tis the way of it. Some people are sick from the moment they set foot on deck." The man, striding toward them, voice booming, had a huge barrel chest and a florid, meaty face that contrasted dramatically with his dark blue coat and golden epaulets. "I am sorry to say it, but your reaction bodes ill for how you will fare during the voyage, mademoiselle. I can tell you that though I have lost passengers to the sea, I have never lost one to seasickness."

"I—I think I will be better if I can get below," Lenobia said quickly, hyperaware that with each moment the Bishop was getting closer and closer to boarding.

"Oh, poor Cecile," Sister Marie Madeleine murmured. Then added, "Girls, this is our captain, Commodore William Cornwallis. He is a great patriot and will keep us quite safe during our long journey."

"That is very kind of you to say, good Sister." The Commodore motioned at a plainly dressed, young mulatto man who was standing nearby. "Martin, show the ladies to their quarters."

"*Merci beaucoup,* Commodore," said Sister Marie Madeleine.

"I hope to see you all at dinner this evening." The big man gave Lenobia a little wink. "At least those of you with the stomach to attend! Excuse me, ladies." He strode away, bellowing at a group of crew members who were struggling awkwardly with a large crate.

"Mademoiselles, madame, if you would follow me," Martin said.

Lenobia was the first to fall in line behind the broadshouldered form of Martin as he nimbly led them through a door in the rear of the deck and down a rather treacherously narrow stairwell that led to an almost equally narrow hallway branching to the left and right. Martin jerked his chin toward the left and Lenobia caught a glimpse of his strong, young profile. "That way is the crew quarters." As he spoke there was a loud crashing sound and a highpitched squeal coming from the direction in which his chin had pointed.

"Crew?" Lenobia couldn't help asking with a lift of her brows, the familiar sound of an annoyed horse momentarily making her forget to be mute and invisible.

Martin looked down at her. A smile tilted the corners of his lips up and his eyes, which were an unusual light olive green, sparkled. Lenobia couldn't tell whether the sparkle was humor, mischief, or sarcasm. He said, "Down the deck below the crews' quarters be the cargo, and in the cargo there be the pair of grays Vincent Rillieux purchased for his carriage."

"Grays?" Simonette asked, but she wasn't peeking down

the long hallway—she was peering with open curiosity at Martin.

"Horses," Lenobia said.

"Percherons, a matched set of geldings," Martin corrected. "Giant brutes. Not for ladies. Dark and damp it be in the cargo hold. No place for ladies or gentlemen proper," he said, meeting Lenobia's gaze with a frankness that surprised her before he turned to the right and continued to talk as he walked. "This way is your quarters. There be four rooms for you to divide up. The Commodore and any male passengers is above you."

Simonette wrapped her arm through Lenobia's and whispered in a rush, "I have never seen a mulatto before. I wonder if they are all so handsome as this one!"

"Sssh!" Lenobia hushed her just as Martin stopped before the first room that opened to the right off the narrow hallway.

"That will be all. Thank you, Martin." Sister Marie Madeleine had caught up with them and gave Simonette a hard look as she dismissed the mulatto.

"Yes, Sister," he said as he bowed to the nun and began back down the hallway.

"*Excuse moi*, Martin. Where and when do we dine with the Commodore?" Sister Marie Madeleine asked.

Martin paused in his retreat to answer. "Commodore's

table is where you have dinner, at seven o'clock each night. Prompt, madame. The Commodore, he insist on formal dress. Other meals be brought to you." Though Martin's tone had turned gruff, when his glance went to Lenobia she thought his expression was more filled with a shy curiosity than mean-spiritedness.

"Will we be the only guests at the Commodore's dinner?" Lenobia asked.

"Surely he will include the Bishop in his invitation," said Sister Marie Madeleine briskly.

"Oh, *oui,* the Bishop will attend. He also perform Mass. The Commodore is a proper Catholic, as are the crew, madame," Martin assured her before disappearing from sight down the hallway.

This time, Lenobia did not have to pretend that she felt ill.

"No, no, truly. Please go without me. A little bread, cheese, and watered wine are all I need," Lenobia assured Sister Marie Madeleine.

"Mademoiselle Cecile, would the company of the Commodore and the Bishop not take your mind off the upset of your stomach?" The nun frowned as she hesitated at the doorway with the other girls, all dressed and eager for their first dinner at the Commodore's table.

"No!" Thinking of what would happen if the Bishop recognized her, Lenobia knew her face had gone pale. She gagged a little and pressed her hand to her mouth as if holding back the sickness. "I cannot even bear the thought of food. I should certainly embarrass myself with sickness if I attempted it."

Sister Marie Madeleine sighed heavily. "Very well. Rest for this evening. I will bring you back some bread and cheese."

"Thank you, Sister."

"I am quite certain you will be yourself tomorrow," Simonette called before Sister Marie Madeleine closed the door gently behind her.

Lenobia let out a long breath and tossed back the hood of her cloak along with her silver-blond hair. Not wasting any of her precious time alone, she dragged the large chest that was engraved in gold with CECILE MARSON DE LA TOUR

D'AUVERGNE over to the far side of the room near the sleeping pallet she had chosen for herself. Lenobia positioned the trunk under one of the round portholes and then she climbed atop it, pulled the little brass hook that held the glass closed, and breathed deeply of the cool, moist air.

The thick trunk made her just tall enough to see out of the window. In awe, Lenobia gazed at the endless expanse of water. It was past dusk, but there was still enough light in the enormous sky for the waves to be illuminated. Lenobia didn't think she'd ever seen anything as mesmerizing as the ocean at night. Her body swayed gracefully with the movement of the ship. Sick? Absolutely not!

"But I will pretend to be," she whispered aloud to the ocean and the night. "Even if I must keep up the pretense for the full eight weeks of the voyage."

Eight weeks! The thought of it was terrible. She had gasped in shock when the always-chattering Simonette had remarked how hard it was to believe they would be on this ship for eight whole weeks. Sister Marie Madeleine had given her a strange look, and Lenobia had quickly followed her gasp with a moan, and clutched her stomach.

"I must be more careful," she told herself. "Of course the real Cecile would know that the voyage would take eight weeks. I must be smarter and braver—and most of all I must avoid the Bishop."

She reluctantly closed the little window, stepped down, and opened the trunk. As she reached in to begin searching through the expensive silks and laces for a sleeping shift, she found a folded piece of paper lying atop the glittering mound. The name *Cecile* was written in her mother's distinctively bold script. Lenobia's hands shook only a little when she opened the letter and read:

My daughter,
You are betrothed to the Duc of Silegne's youngest son,
Thinton de Silegne. He is master of a large plantation
one day's ride north of New Orleans. I do not know if
he is kind or handsome, only that he is young, rich, and
comes from a fine family. I will pray with every sunrise
that you find happiness and that your children know
how fortunate they are to have such a brave woman as
their mother.

Your maman

Lenobia closed her eyes, wiped the tears from her cheeks, and clutched her mother's letter. It was a sign that all would be well! She was going to marry a man who lived a day's ride north of where the Bishop would be. Surely a large, rich plantation would have its own chapel. If it didn't, Lenobia would make quite certain it soon would.

All she had to do was avoid discovery until she left New Orleans.

It shouldn't be so difficult, she told herself. *For the past two years I have been avoiding the prying eyes of men. In comparison, eight more weeks is not long at all . . .*

Much later, when Lenobia allowed herself to remember that fateful voyage, she considered the oddness of time, and how eight weeks could pass at such differing speeds.

The first two days had seemed interminable. Sister Marie Madeleine hovered around her, trying to tempt her to eat—which was a torture because Lenobia was absolutely ravenous and wanted to sink her teeth into the biscuits and hot sliced pork that the good nun kept offering her. Instead she nibbled on some hard bread and drank watered wine until her cheeks felt hot and her head was spinning.

Just after dawn of the third day, the ocean, which had been placid, changed utterly and became an angry gray entity that tossed the *Minerva* to and fro as if she were a twig. The Commodore made a grand show of coming to their rooms and assuring them that the squall was comparatively mild and, in actuality, fortuitous—that it was pushing them toward New Orleans at a much faster rate than was typical for this time of year.

Lenobia was pleased about that, but she thought it even more fortuitous that the rough seas caused more than half of her shipmates—including the poor, unfortunate Bishop—to become violently ill and to keep to their quarters. Lenobia felt bad for being relieved at so much sickness, but it certainly made the next ten days easier for her. And by the time the sea had become placid again, Lenobia's pattern of preferring to keep to herself had been well established. Except for occasional bursts of Simonette's irrepressible chattering, the other girls mostly left Lenobia to herself.

At first she'd thought she'd be lonely. Lenobia did miss her mother badly, but it was a surprise to her how much she enjoyed the solitude—the time alone with her thoughts. But that was just the first of her surprises. The truth was, until her secret was discovered, Lenobia had found happiness, and it was due to three things—sunrise and horses—and the young man she'd chanced upon because of them.

She'd found the way to the Percherons the same way she'd discovered how peaceful and private it was in the wee hours just before and during the rising of the sun—by finding the path least frequented by the rest of the people aboard.

None of the other girls ever left her sleeping pallet before the sun was well into the morning sky. Sister Marie Madeleine was always the first of the women awake. She rose when dawn's light changed from pink to yellow, and went immediately to the little shrine she'd created for the Virgin Mary, lit one precious candle, and began praying. The nun also came to her altar mid-morning for Marian litanies, and to recite the Little Office of the Virgin before she went to bed, instructing the girls to pray with her. In truth, every morning the devout Sister prayed so fervently—eyes closed, counting her rosary beads by touch—that it was a simple thing to slip into or out of the room without disturbing her.

That was how it began—Lenobia's pattern of waking before all the others and roaming silently around the ship, finding pockets of solitude and so much more beauty than she had ever imagined. She'd been going mad, stuck in that one room, hiding from the Bishop and pretending to be ill. Early one morning, when all the girls, even Sister Marie Madeleine, were sound asleep, she'd taken a chance and tiptoed from the chamber and into the hallway. The sea was rough—the squall just really setting in—but Lenobia had no trouble keeping to her feet. She enjoyed the pitch and roll of the *Minerva*. She also enjoyed the fact that the bad weather was keeping even many of the crew in their quarters.

Listening as hard as she could, Lenobia had moved from shadow to shadow, making her way up to a dark corner of the deck. There she'd stood near the railing and breathed great gulps of fresh air while she stared out at the water and the sky and the vast expanse of emptiness. She hadn't been thinking anything—she'd just been feeling the freedom.

And then something amazing happened.

The sky had changed from coal and gray to blush and peach, primrose and saffron. The crystal waters magnified all those colors, and Lenobia had been captivated by the majesty of it. Yes, of course, she had often been awake at dawn at the château, but she'd always been busy. She'd never had time to sit and watch the lightening of the sky and the magickal lifting of the sun from a distant horizon.

From that morning on it became part of her own religious ritual, and Lenobia was, in her own way, as devout as was Sister Marie Madeleine. Each dawn she would steal above deck, find a spot of shadow and solitude, and watch the sky welcome the sun.

And as she did, Lenobia gave thanks for the beauty she had been allowed to witness. Holding her mother's rosary beads, she prayed fervently that she be allowed to see another dawn in safety, with her secret undiscovered. She would stay above deck as long as she dared, until the noises of the waking crew drove her back below, where she slipped into her shared room and went back to the charade of being an ill, delicate loner.

It was just after she'd watched her third dawn and she was retracing what had become the familiar path to her room that Lenobia found the horses, and then him. She'd heard the men coming up from below just as she was about to enter the stairwell hallway, and had been almost certain that one of the voices—the one that was gruffest of them all—had belonged to the Bishop. Her reaction was immediate. Lenobia lifted her skirts and ran as quickly and silently as possible in the opposite direction. She flitted from shadow to shadow, always moving away from the voices. She didn't pause when she found the little arched doorway that led to steep, narrow stairs dropping down and down like a ladder. She simply climbed down until she came to the bottom.

Lenobia smelled them before she saw them. The scents of horse and hay and manure were as familiar as they were comforting. She probably should have paused there only a moment—she was quite certain none of the other girls would have paid so much as an instant's attention to the horses. But Lenobia was not like other girls. She had always loved animals—all types of animals, but especially horses.

Their sounds and scents drew her as the moon drew the tide. There was a surprising amount of light filtering from large rectangular openings in the deck above, and it was easy for Lenobia to make her way around crates and sacks, bushels and barrels, until she was standing before a makeshift stall. Two huge gray heads hung over the half wall, ears pricked attentively in her direction.

"Ooooh! Look at the two of you! You're exquisite!" Lenobia went to them, moving carefully and not making any silly, abrupt motions that might spook them. But she needn't have worried. The pair of Percherons seemed as curious about her as she was about them. She held her hands out to them and both began blowing against her palms. She rubbed their broad foreheads and kissed their soft muzzles, giggling girlishly as they lipped her hair.

The giggle was what made Lenobia realize the truth—that she was actually feeling a bubble of happiness. And that was something she hadn't believed she would ever truly feel again. Oh, she would certainly feel the satisfaction and safety that living the life of a legitimate daughter of a baron would bring her. She hoped that she might feel contentment, if not love for Thinton de Silegne, the man she had been fated to marry in Cecile's place. But happiness? Lenobia hadn't expected to feel happiness.

She smiled as one of the horses lipped the lace on the

sleeve of her dress. "Horses and happiness—they go to-gether," she told the gelding.

It was while she was standing between the two Perche-rons, feeling that unexpected bubble of happiness, that a huge black and white cat jumped from the top of the near-est crate and landed with a monstrous thud near her feet.

Lenobia and the Percherons startled. The horses arched their necks and sent the feline wary looks.

"I know," Lenobia said to them. "I agree with you. That is the biggest cat I have ever seen."

As if on cue, the cat flopped over onto its back, curled its head around, and blinked innocent green eyes up at Lenobia while rumbling a strange, low *rrrrow*.

Lenobia looked at the geldings. They looked at her. She shrugged and said, "*Oui*, it seems he wants his stomach scratched." She smiled and reached down.

"I would not do that, you."

Lenobia pulled her hand back and froze. Heart pound-ing, she felt trapped and guilty as the man stepped from the shadows. Recognizing Martin, the mulatto who had shown them to their quarters just days before, she breathed a small sigh of relief and tried to look less guilty and more lady-like.

"She seems to want her stomach scratched," Lenobia said.

"He," Martin corrected with a wry smile. "Odysseus is using his favorite ruse on you, mademoiselle." He plucked a long piece of hay from one of the nearby bales of alfalfa and tickled it against the cat's plump stomach. Odysseus promptly closed on the hay, capturing it and biting it thoroughly before speeding off to disappear among the cargo. "It is his game. He looks harmless to lure you in, and then he attacks."

"Is he really mean?"

Martin shrugged broad shoulders. "I think not mean that one, just mischievous. But what do I know—I am not a learned gentleman or a great lady."

Lenobia almost responded automatically, "Neither am I!" Thankfully, Martin continued. "Mademoiselle, this is no place for a lady. You will soil your clothing and muss your hair." She thought that even though Martin was speaking in a respectful, appropriate manner, there was something about his look—his tone—that was dismissive and patronizing. And that annoyed her. Not because she was supposed to be above his class. Lenobia cared because she was not one of those rich, pampered, snobbish mademoiselles who belittled others and knew nothing about hard work. She was not Cecile Marson de La Tour d'Auvergne.

Lenobia narrowed her eyes at him. "I like horses." To punctuate her point, she stepped back between the two grays and patted their thick necks. "I also like cats—even mischievous ones. And I do not mind having my clothing soiled or my hair mussed."

Lenobia saw the surprise in his expressive green eyes, but before he could reply the sound of men's voices drifted down from above.

"I must get back. I cannot get caught"—Lenobia stopped herself before she could blurt "by the Bishop," and instead finished hastily—"roaming the ship. I should be in my quarters. I—I have not been well."

"I remember," Martin said. "You looked ill as soon as you came aboard. You do not look so bad now, even though the sea is rough today."

"Walking around makes me feel better, but Sister Marie Madeleine does not think it appropriate." Actually, the good Sister hadn't made that exact pronunciation. She hadn't had to. All of the girls seemed content to sit and embroider or gossip or play one of the two precious harpsichords being shipped with them. None of them had shown any interest in exploring the grand ship.

"The Sister—she a strong woman. I think even the Commodore a little afraid of her," he said.

"I know, I know, but, well, I just . . . I like seeing the rest of the ship." Lenobia struggled to find the right words that would not betray too much.

Martin nodded. "The other mademoiselles rarely leave their quarters. Some of us, we think they might be *fille à la casquette*, the casket girls." He said the phrase in French and then English, eerily echoing her mother's comment to her the day she'd left the château. He cocked his head and studied her, rubbing his chin in exaggerated concentration. "You don' look much like a casket girl, you."

"*Exactement!* That is what I am trying to tell you. I am not like the other girls." As male voices drifted closer and closer, Lenobia stroked each of the grays in farewell, then swallowed her fear and turned to face the young man. "Please, Martin, will you show me how to get back without going through there," she pointed to the ladder-like stairwell she'd climbed down, "and having to cross the entire deck?"

"*Oui,*" he said with only a slight hesitation.

"And will you promise to tell no one that I have been here? Please?"

"*Oui,*" he repeated. "*Allons-y.*"

Martin led her quickly in a twisting path through the mountains of cargo all the way across the underbelly of the ship until they came to a larger, more accessible entrance. "Up there," Martin explained. "Keep going up. It will lead you to the hallway of your quarters."

"It goes past the crew's quarters, too, does it not?"

"It does. If you see men you raise your chin, thus." Martin lifted his chin. "Then you give to them the look you gave to me when you tell me you like horse, and cats of mischief. They will not bother you."

"Thank you, Martin! Thank you so much," Lenobia said.

"Do you know why I help you?"

Martin's question had her turning back to look at him questioningly. "I suppose it is because you must be a man with a good heart."

Martin shook his head. "No, it is because you were brave enough to ask it of me."

The giggle that escaped Lenobia's mouth was semi-hysterical. "Brave? No, I am frightened of everything!"

He smiled. "Except horses and cats."

She returned his smile, feeling her cheeks get warm and her stomach make a little fluttery shiver because his smile made him even more handsome. "Yes." Lenobia tried to pretend she wasn't breathless. "Except horses and cats. Thank you, again, Martin."

She was almost through the doorway when he added, "I feed the horses. Every morning just after dawn."

Cheeks still warm, Lenobia glanced back at him. "Perhaps I will see you again."

His green eyes sparkled and he tipped an imaginary hat to her. "Perhaps, *cherie,* perhaps."

CHAPTER FOUR

For the next four weeks Lenobia existed in an odd state that was somewhere between peace and anxiety, happiness and despair. Time played with her. The hours that she sat in her quarters waiting for dusk and then night and then the gloaming of predawn seemed to take an eternity to pass. But as soon as the ship slept and she was able to slip the confines of her self-imposed prison, the next few hours rushed past, leaving her breathless and yearning for more.

She would prowl the ship, soaking in freedom with the salt air, watching the sun burst gloriously from the watery horizon, and then she would slip down to the joy that awaited her below deck.

For a little while she convinced herself it was only the grays that made her so happy—so eager to rush to the cargo hold and so sad when the time passed too quickly; the ship began to wake, and she had to return to her quarters.

It couldn't have anything to do with Martin's broad shoulders or his smile or the sparkle in his olive-colored eyes and the way he teased her and made her laugh.

"Those grays don' be eating that bread you bring them. No one be eating that stuff," he'd said, chuckling that first morning she'd returned.

She'd frowned. "They will eat it because it is so salty. Horses like salty things." She'd held the hard bread out, one piece in each palm, and offered it to the Percherons. They'd sniffed and then, with surprising delicacy for such big animals, taken the bread and chewed with a lot of head bobbing and expressions of surprise that had made Lenobia and Martin laugh together.

"You were right, *cher*!" Martin said. "How you know about what horses like to eat, a lady like you?"

"My father has many horses. I told you I like them. So I spent time in the stables," she said evasively.

"And your *père*, he not mind that his daughter is in the stables?"

"My father did not pay attention to where I was," she said, thinking that, at least, was the truth. "What about you? Where did you learn about horses?" Lenobia changed the focus of their conversation.

"The Rillieux plantation just outside New Orleans."

"Yes, that was the name of the man you said was shipping the grays. So, Monsieur Rillieux must trust you quite a lot if he sent you to travel all the way to and from New Orleans and France with his horses."

"He should, he. Monsieur Rillieux is my father."

"Your father? But, I thought—" Her words trailed off and Lenobia felt her cheeks getting hot.

"You thought because my skin is brown my *père* could not be white?"

Lenobia thought he seemed more amused than offended, so she took a chance and said what was on her mind. "No, I know one of your parents had to be white. The Commodore called you a mulatto, and your skin is not really brown. It is lighter than that. It is more like cream with just a small bit of chocolate mixed with it." To herself Lenobia thought, *His skin is more beautiful than plain white could ever possibly be,* and felt her cheeks flame again.

"Quadroon, *cherie,*" Martin said, smiling into her eyes.

"Quadroon?"

"*Oui,* that is me. My maman, she was Rillieux's first *placage*. She was a mulatto."

"*Placage*? I do not understand."

"Rich white men take women of color in the *marriages de la main gauche*."

"Left-handed marriages?"

"Means not real by law, but real for New Orleans. That

was my maman, only she die not long after my birth. Rillieux keep me on and have his slaves raise me."

"Are you a slave?"

"No. I am Creole. Free man of color. I work for Rillieux." When Lenobia just stared at him, trying to take in everything she was learning, he smiled and said, "Since you here you want to help me groom the grays, or you scurry back to your room like a proper lady."

Lenobia lifted her chin. "Since I am here—I stay. And I will help you."

The next hour sped by quickly. The Percherons were a lot of horse to groom, and Lenobia had been busy, working with Martin and talking about nothing more personal than horses and arguing the pros and cons of tail docking, even though the whole time she could not stop thinking about *placage* and *marriages de la main gauche*.

It was only as Lenobia began to leave that she was able to have the courage to ask Martin the question that had been circling around in her mind. "The *placage*—do the women get to choose, or do they have to be with whomever wants them?"

"There are many kinds of people, *cherie*, and many kinds of arrangements, but from what I see it is more about choice and love than not."

"Good," Lenobia said. "I am glad for them."

"You had no choice, did you, *cher*?" Martin asked, meeting her gaze.

"I did what my mother told me to do," she said truthfully, and then she left the cargo hold and carried the scent of horses and the memory of olive eyes with her throughout the tedium of that long day.

What began as accident became habit, and something she rationalized as being just for the horses became her joy—what she needed to get through the never-ending voyage. Lenobia couldn't wait to see Martin—to hear what he would say next—to talk with him about her dreams and even her fears. She didn't mean to confide in him—to like him—to care for him at all, but she did. How could she not? Martin was funny and smart and beautiful—so very beautiful.

"You getting skinny, you," he said to her on the fifth day.

"What are talking about? I have always been petite." Lenobia paused as she combed through the tangled mane of one of the geldings and peeked around his arched neck at Martin. "I am not skinny," she said firmly.

"Skinny, *cher*. That what you are." He ducked under the gelding's neck and was suddenly there, beside her, close and warm and solid. He took her wrist gently in his hand and circled it easily with his forefinger and thumb. "See there? You all bone."

His touch shocked her. He was tall and muscular but gentle. His movements were slow, steady, almost hypnotic. It was as if his every motion was made deliberately, so as not to frighten her. Unexpectedly he reminded her of a Percheron. His thumb stroked the inside of her wrist, over her pulse point.

"I have to pretend not to want to eat," she heard herself admitting.

"Why, *cher*?"

"It is better for me if I stay away from everyone, and being sick gives me a reason to keep to myself."

"Everyone? Why don' you stay away from me?" he asked boldly.

Even though her heart felt as if it would pound from her

chest, she pulled her wrist from his gentle grip and gave him a stern look. "I come for the horses and not for you."

"Ah, *les chevaux*. Of course." He stroked the neck of the gelding, but he didn't smile as she expected, nor did he joke back with her. Instead he just looked at her, as if he could see through her tough façade to the softness of her heart. He said no more and instead handed her one of the thick curry brushes from a nearby bucket. "He likes this one best."

"Thank you," she said, and began working her way across the broad body of the gelding with the brush.

There was only a small, uncomfortable silence and then Martin's voice carried from the other side of the gelding he was tending. "So, *cherie,* what story I tell you today? The one about how anything you plant in the black dirt of New France grows taller than these *petite chevaux*, or about the pearls in the *tignons* of the beautiful *placage* and how the women they stroll through the square?"

"Tell me about the women—about the *placage*," Lenobia said, and then she listened eagerly as Martin painted pictures in her imagination of gorgeous women who were free enough to choose whom they would love, though not free enough to make their unions legal.

Then next morning when she rushed into the cargo

hold she found him already grooming the horses. A hunk of cheese and fragrant hot pork between two thick slices of fresh bread sat on a clean cloth near the barrels of oats. Without glancing at her, Martin said, "Eat, *cherie*. You don' pretend around me."

Perhaps that was the morning it changed for Lenobia and she began to think of it as seeing Martin at dawn rather than visiting the horses at dawn. Or, more precisely, perhaps that was when she began to admit the change to herself.

And once it changed for her, Lenobia began searching for signs from Martin that she was more than just his friend— more than *ma cherie,* the girl he brought food to and who pestered him for stories of New France. But all she found in his gaze was familiar kindness. All she heard in his voice was patience and humor. Once or twice she thought she caught a glimmer of more, especially when they laughed together and the olive green in his eyes seemed to sparkle with flecks of golden brown, but he always turned away if she met his gaze too long, and he always had a humorous story ready if the silences between them became too great.

Just before the small measure of peace and happiness she'd found shattered and her world exploded, Lenobia finally found the courage to ask the question that would not allow her to sleep. It was as she was brushing off her skirts and whispering to the nearest gelding an affectionate *a bientôt* that she took a deep breath and said, "Martin, I need to ask you a question."

"What is it, *cherie*?" he responded absently while he gathered up the curry brushes and linen rags they'd used to wipe down the geldings.

"You tell me stories of the women like your maman—women of color who become *placage* and live as wives to white men. But what of men of color being with white women? What of male *placage*?"

From outside the stall his gaze went to hers and she saw his surprise and then amusement, and she knew he was going to humiliate her by laughing. Then he truly looked into her eyes, and his teasing response turned somber. He shook his head slowly from side to side. His voice sounded weary and his broad shoulders seemed to slump. "No, *cherie*. There are no male *placage*. Only way a man of color can be with a white woman is if he leave New France and pass as white."

"Pass as white?" Lenobia felt breathless at her boldness. "You mean to pretend you are white?"

"*Oui*, but not me, *cherie*." Martin held out his arm. It was long and muscular and, in the postdawn light filtering from the deck above, it looked more bronze than brown. "This skin too brown to pass, and I think I am not one for being any more, or less, than I am. Nah, *cherie*. I be happy in my own skin." Their gazes held and Lenobia tried to tell him with a look all that she was beginning to wish—all that she was beginning to want. "I see a storm in those gray eyes of yours, *cherie*. You leave that storm be. You strong, you. But not strong enough to change the way the world think—the way the world believe."

Lenobia didn't reply until she'd opened the little half door and exited the Percherons' stall. She went to Martin, smoothed her skirt, and then looked up into his eyes. "Even the New World?" Her voice was barely above a whisper.

"*Cherie,* we do not speak of it, but I know you one of the *fille à la casquette*. You promised to a great man. That true, *cherie*?"

"It is true. His name is Thinton de Silegne," she said. "He is a name with no face—no body—no heart."

"He a name with land, though, *cherie*. I know his name and his land. His plantation, the Houmas, is like paradise."

"It is not paradise I want, Martin. It is only y—"

"No!" He stopped her, pressing a finger against her lips. "You cannot speak it, you. My heart, he is strong, but not strong enough to fight your words."

Lenobia took his hand from her lips and held it in hers. It felt warm and rough, like there was nothing he couldn't defeat or defend with that hand. "I only ask that your heart listen."

"Oh, *cherie*. My heart, he already heard your words.

Your heart, she speak them to me. But that as far as they can go—only this silent talk between us."

"But . . . I want more," she said.

"*Oui, mon petite chou,* I want more, too. But it cannot be. Cecile, we cannot be."

That was the first time he'd called her by that name since she'd been coming to him at dawn, and the sound of it took her aback, so much so that she dropped his hand and stepped away from him.

He thinks I am Cecile, the legitimate daughter of a baron. Do I tell him? Would it matter? "I—I should go." She stumbled over the words, completely overwhelmed by the conflicting layers of her life. Lenobia started toward the large cargo deck exit. Behind her, Martin spoke.

"You not come back here again, *cherie.*"

Lenobia looked over her shoulder at him. "Are you saying you do not want me to come back?"

"I could not speak that lie to you," he said.

Lenobia breathed a long, trembling sigh of relief before saying, "Then if you are asking me, my answer is yes. I will come back here again. Tomorrow. At dawn. Nothing has changed."

She continued walking out, and heard the echo of his voice following her, saying, "Everything has changed, *ma cherie* . . ."

Lenobia's thoughts were in tumult. Had everything changed between them?

Yes. Martin said his heart heard my words. But what did that mean? She climbed the narrow stairwell and entered the hallway that ran from the cargo entrance past the crew's quarters, the deck access way, and then ended at the female passengers' quarters. She hurried past the crew doorway. It was later than she usually returned, and she heard hardly any sounds of crew members rustling about within, getting ready to begin the day. She should have known then that she needed to be more careful. She should have stopped and listened, but all Lenobia could hear was the sound of her thoughts answering her own question: *What did it mean that Martin said his heart heard my words? It meant that he knows I love him.*

I love him. I love Martin.

It was as she admitted that to herself that the Bishop, purple robes swirling around him, moved into the hallway not two steps behind her.

"Bonjour, mademoiselle," he said.

Had Lenobia been less distracted, she would have immediately ducked her head, curtseyed, and scampered back to the safety of her quarters. Instead she made a terrible mistake. Lenobia looked up at him.

Their gazes met. "Ah, it is the little mademoiselle who

has been so ill all voyage." He paused and she saw confusion in his dark eyes. He even tilted his head and furrowed his brow as he studied her. "But I thought you were the Baron d'Auvergne's . . ." His voice trailed off as his eyes widened in recognition and then understanding.

"*Bonjour,* Father." She spoke quickly, ducked her head, curtseyed, and tried to retreat. But it was too late. The Bishop's hand snaked out and grabbed her arm.

"I know your pretty face, and it is not that of Cecile Marson de La Tour d'Auvergne, daughter of the Baron d'Auvergne."

"No, please. Let me go, Father." Lenobia tried to pull away from him, but his hot grip felt stronger than iron.

"I know your pretty, pretty face," he repeated. His surprise turned to a cruel smile. "You are a daughter of the Baron, but you are his *fille de bas.* Everyone near the Château de Navarre knows of the succulent little fruit that dropped from the wrong side of the Baron's tree."

His bastard daughter . . . succulent little fruit . . . wrong side . . . The words battered her, filling her with dread. Lenobia shook her head back and forth, back and forth. "No, I must return to my quarters. Sister Marie Madeleine will be missing me."

"As indeed I have been."

The Bishop and Lenobia were startled by the sound of Sister Marie Madeleine's commanding voice—he enough that Lenobia was able to pull loose from him and stumble down the hall to the nun.

"What is this about, Father?" Sister Marie Madeleine asked. But before the Bishop could answer her, the nun touched Lenobia's cheek and said, "Cecile, why are you trembling so? Have you been ill again?"

"You call her Cecile? Are you in on this unholy masquerade?" The Bishop seemed to fill the hallway as he loomed over the two women.

Clearly not intimidated, Sister Marie Madeleine stepped forward, putting herself between Lenobia and the priest. "I have no idea of what you speak, Father, but you are frightening this child."

"This child is a bastard impostor!" the Bishop roared.

"Father! Have you gone quite mad?" the nun said, drawing back as if he'd struck her.

"Do you know? Is that why you have kept her hidden for the entire voyage?" The Bishop continued to rage. Lenobia could hear the sounds of doors opening behind her and she knew the other girls were coming into the hallway. She could not look at them—she would not look at them. "This is a travesty! I will excommunicate both of you. The Holy Father himself will hear of this!"

Lenobia could see the curious looks the crewmen were giving them as the Bishop's tirade drew more and more attention. And then, far down the hallway behind the Bishop, Lenobia caught sight of Martin's startled face and saw that he was coming toward her.

It was terrible enough that Sister Marie Madeleine was standing there, protecting and believing in her. She couldn't bear it if Martin were somehow pulled into the mess she had made of her life as well.

"No!" Lenobia cried, moving around Sister Marie Madeleine. "I did this on my own. No one knew, no one! Especially not the good Sister."

"What is it the child has done?" the Commodore asked as he stepped into the hallway, frowning from the Bishop to Lenobia.

The Bishop opened his mouth to shout her sin, but before he could speak, Lenobia confessed. "I am not Cecile Marson de La Tour d'Auvergne. Cecile died the morning the carriage came to take her to Le Havre. I am another daughter of the Baron d'Auvergne—his bastard daughter. I took Cecile's place without anyone at the château knowing because I wanted a better life for myself." Lenobia met the nun's gaze steadily. "I am sorry I lied to you, Sister. Please forgive me."

CHAPTER FIVE

"No, gentlemen, I must insist you leave the girl to me. She is a *fille à la casquette,* and as such is under the protection of the Ursuline nuns." Sister Marie Madeleine positioned herself in the doorway to their room, holding the door half closed before her. She had told Lenobia to go immediately to her pallet and then had squared off against the Bishop and the Commodore, who hovered in the hallway. The Bishop was still blustering and red-faced. The Commodore didn't seem to know how to look—he appeared to vacillate between anger and humor. As the nun spoke, the military man shrugged and said, "Yes, well, she is your charge, Sister."

"She is a bastard and an impostor!" the Bishop said.

"Bastard she is—impostor she is no more," the nun said firmly. "She has admitted her sin and asked for forgiveness. Is it not now our job as good Catholics to forgive and help the child find her true path in life?"

"You could not possibly believe I would allow you to marry that little bastard to a nobleman!" said the Bishop.

"And you could not possibly believe I would involve myself in deceit and break my vow of honesty," the nun countered.

Lenobia thought she could feel the heat of the Bishop's anger all the way across the room.

"Then what are you going to do with her?" he asked.

"I am going to complete my charge and be certain she arrives in New Orleans safe and chaste. From there it will be up to the Ursuline Council and, of course, the child herself, as to her future."

"That sounds reasonable," said the Commodore. "Come, Charles, let us leave the women to women's dealings. I have a case of excellent port that we have not yet opened. Let us sample it and be sure it has survived the voyage thus far." Giving the Sister a dismissive nod, he clapped the Bishop on his shoulder before walking away.

The purple-robed man didn't immediately follow the Commodore. Instead he looked past Sister Marie Madeleine to where Lenobia sat, arms hugging herself, on her pallet. "God's holy fire burns out liars," he said.

"I think God's holy fire does not burn out children, though. Good day to you, Father," Sister Marie Madeleine said, and then she closed the door in the priest's face.

The room was so quiet Lenobia could hear Simonette's excited little breaths.

Lenobia met Sister Marie Madeleine's gaze. "I am sorry," she said.

The nun raised her hand. "First, let us begin with your name. Your real name."

"Lenobia Whitehall." For a moment the rush of relief at being able to reclaim her name overshadowed fear and shame, and she was able to draw a deep, fortifying breath. "That is my real name."

"How could you do it? Pretend to be a poor, dead girl?" Simonette said. She was staring at Lenobia with huge eyes as if she were an unusual and frightening species of creature newly discovered.

Lenobia glanced at the nun. The Sister nodded, saying, "They will all want to know. Answer now and be through with it."

"I did not so much pretend to be Cecile, but rather I simply kept quiet." Lenobia looked at Simonette, dressed in her silks trimmed in sable, pearls and garnets twinkling around her slim, white neck. "You do not know what it is to have nothing—no protection—no future. I did not want to be Cecile. I just wanted to be safe and happy."

"But you are a bastard," said Aveline de Lafayette, the beautiful blonde youngest daughter of the Marquis de

Lafayette. "You do not deserve the life of a legitimate daughter."

"How could you believe such nonsense?" Lenobia said. "Why should an accident of birth decide the worth of a person?"

"God decides our worth," said Sister Marie Madeleine.

"And last time I checked, you were not God, mademoiselle," Lenobia said to the young de Lafayette.

Aveline gasped. "This daughter of a whore will not speak to me like that!"

"My mother is not a whore! She is a woman who was too beautiful and too trusting!"

"Of course you would say that, but we already know you are a liar." Aveline de Lafayette picked up her skirts and began to brush past Lenobia, saying, "Sister, I will not share a room with a *fille de bas.*"

"Enough!" The sharpness of the nun's voice had even the arrogant de Lafayette pausing. "Aveline, at the Ursuline convent we educate women. We make no distinction between class or race in doing so. What is important is that we treat everyone with honesty and respect. Lenobia has given us honesty. We will return that with respect." The nun shifted her gaze to Lenobia. "I can listen to the confession of your sin, but I cannot absolve you of that sin. For that you need a priest."

Lenobia shuddered. "I will not confess to the Bishop."

Marie Madeleine's expression softened. "Begin by confessing to God, child. Then our good Father Pierre at the convent will hear your confession when we arrive." Her gaze moved from Lenobia to each of the other girls in the room. "Father Pierre would hear any of your confessions because we are each imperfect and in need of absolution." She turned back to Lenobia. "Child, would you join me on deck, please?"

Lenobia nodded silently and followed the Sister above. They walked the short way up to the aft part of the ship and stood beside the black railing and ornately carved cherubic figures that decorated the rear of the *Minerva*. They stood without speaking for a few moments, each woman looking out to sea and keeping to her own thoughts. Lenobia knew being discovered as an impostor would change her life, probably for the worse, but she couldn't help feeling a small thrill of release—of freedom from the lie that had been haunting her.

"I hated the lie." She heard herself speak her thought aloud.

"I am glad to hear you say it. You do not seem a deceitful girl to me." Marie Madeleine moved her gaze to Lenobia. "Tell me truly, did no one else know of your ruse?"

Lenobia did not expect the question and she looked

away, not able to say the truth and not willing to tell another lie.

"Ah, I see. Your maman, she knew," Marie Madeleine said, not unkindly. "No matter, what is done cannot be undone. I will not ask you about it again."

"Thank you, Sister," Lenobia said quietly.

The nun paused, and then with a sharper tone continued. "You should have come to me when you first saw the Bishop instead of pretending illness."

"I did not know what you would do," Lenobia said honestly.

"I am not quite certain myself, but I do know I would have done everything in my power to avert an ugly confrontation with the Bishop such as the one we had today." The nun's gaze was sharp and clear. "What is it that is between the two of you?"

"Nothing on my part!" Lenobia said quickly, then sighed and added, "Some time ago, my maman, who is devout, said that we would no longer go to Mass. Instead she kept me home. That did not keep the Bishop from coming to the château—it did not keep his eyes from searching me out."

"Did the Bishop take your maidenhead?"

"No! He did not touch me. I am still a maid."

Marie Madeleine crossed herself. "Thank the Blessed Mother for that." The nun exhaled a long breath. "The

Bishop is a worriment to me. He is not the type of man I would want on the Seat of Saint Louis. But, God's ways are sometimes difficult for us to understand. The voyage will be over in a few weeks, and once we are in New Orleans the Bishop will have many duties to keep him occupied and not thinking of you. So, it is only for a few weeks that we must keep you from the Bishop's eye."

"We?"

Marie Madeleine's brows raised. "Ursuline nuns are servants of the Holy Mother of us all, and She would not want me to stand idly by while one of Her daughters is abused— not even by a Bishop." She brushed away Lenobia's thanks. "You will be expected at dinner now that you have been found out. That cannot be avoided without setting you up for more ridicule and disdain."

"Ridicule and disdain are less offensive than the Bishop's attention," Lenobia said.

"No. They make you more vulnerable to him. You will dine with us. Just call no notice to yourself. Even he cannot do anything in front of the crowd of us. Other than that, even though I am quite sure you are weary of pretending illness and remaining in your quarters, you must stay out of sight."

Lenobia cleared her throat, lifted her chin, and took the plunge. "Sister, for several weeks I have been leaving our quarters before dawn and returning before most of the ship awakens."

The nun smiled. "Yes, child. I know."

"Oh. I thought you were praying."

"Lenobia, I believe you will discover many of my good sisters and I are able to think and pray at the same time. I do appreciate your honesty. Where is it you go?"

"Up here. Well, actually, over there." Lenobia pointed to a shadowy part of the deck where the lifeboats were stored. "I watch the sunrise and walk around a little. And then I go down to the cargo hold."

Marie Madeleine blinked in surprise. "The cargo hold? Whatever for?"

"Horses," Lenobia said. *I am telling the truth,* she rationalized. *Horses drew me there.* "A matched pair of Percherons. I like horses very much, and I am good with them. May I continue visiting them?"

"Do you ever see the Bishop on your dawn outings?"

"No, this was the first morning, and that is only because I stayed out too long after dawn."

The nun shrugged. "As long as you are careful, I see no reason to trap you in your quarters any more than I absolutely must. But do be careful, child."

"I will, *merci beaucoup,* Sister." Impulsively, Lenobia threw her arms around the nun and hugged her. After only a moment strong, motherly arms encircled her in return and the nun patted her shoulder.

"Do not worry, child," Sister Marie Madeleine murmured consolingly. "There is a great shortage of good Catholic girls in New Orleans. We will find you a husband, do not fear."

Trying not to think of Martin, Lenobia whispered, "I would rather you find me a way to earn my living."

The nun was still chuckling as they made their way back to the women's quarters.

In the Commodore's private sitting room, directly below where Lenobia and Marie Madeleine had so recently been speaking, Bishop Charles de Beaumont stood by the open window silent as death, still as a statue. When the Commodore returned from the galley with two dusty bottles of port under his beefy arms, Charles put on a show of being interested in the year and vineyard. He pretended to enjoy the rich wine, when instead he drank deeply and without tasting it, needing to douse the flame of rage that burned so brightly within him while bits and pieces of the conversation he'd overheard boiled through his mind: *What is it that is between the two of you? Did the Bishop take your maidenhead? Ridicule and disdain are less offensive than the Bishop's attention. But do be careful, child . . .*

The Commodore blustered on and on about tides and battle strategies and other such banal subjects and Charles's anger, dampened by wine, simmered slowly and carefully, cooking fully in the juices of hatred and lust and fire—always fire.

The evening meal would have been a disaster had it not been for Sister Marie Madeleine. Simonette was the only girl who would speak to Lenobia, and she did so in awkward starts and stops—as if the fifteen-year-old kept forgetting she wasn't supposed to like Lenobia anymore.

Lenobia concentrated on her food. She thought it was going to be like heaven to be able to eat a full meal, but the Bishop's hot gaze made her feel so sick and scared that she ended up pushing most of the delicious sea bass and buttery potatoes around her plate.

Sister Marie Madeleine made everything work, though. She kept the Commodore engaged in a discussion about the ethics of war that included the Bishop and his ecclesiastical opinions. He couldn't ignore the nun—not when she was showing such obvious interest in the Bishop's opinion. And in much less time than Lenobia would have imagined, the Sister was asking to be excused.

"So soon, madame?" The Commodore blinked blearily at her, face florid from the port. "I was enjoying our conversation very much!"

"Do forgive me, good Commodore, but I wish to go while there is still some light left in the evening sky. The mademoiselles and I should very much like to take a few turns about the deck."

The mademoiselles, obviously shocked by the nun's

proposal, stared at her in varying degrees of surprise and horror.

"Walk? About the deck? And why would you wish to do that, Sister?" asked the Bishop in a sharp voice.

The nun smiled placidly at the Bishop. "*Oui*, I think we have too long been cooped in our rooms." Then she shifted her attention to the Commodore. "Have you not explained many times about the healthful benefits of sea air? And look at you, monsieur, such a big, strong man. We would do well to emulate your habits."

"Ah, indeed, indeed." The Commodore's already massive chest swelled even fuller.

"Excellent! Then with your permission, I am going to recommend the girls and I take frequent walks around the ship at varying times of the day. We must all be mindful of our health, and now that the last of the seasickness has dissolved, there is nothing to keep us to our quarters." Marie Madeleine said the last with a quick, knowing glance at Lenobia, followed by an apologetic look to the Commodore, as if including him in her chagrin at the girl's behavior. Lenobia thought Sister Marie Madeleine was absolutely brilliant.

"Very good, madame. Tip-top idea, really tip-top. Do you not think so, Charles?"

"I think the good Sister is a very wise woman," came the Bishop's sly response.

"It is kind of you to say so, Father," Marie Madeleine said. "And do not let us startle you, as from here out you will never know where any of us could be!"

"I will remember. I will remember." Suddenly the Bishop's stern expression shifted and he blinked as if in surprise. "Sister, I just had a thought that I am quite sure was brought on by your ambitious announcement about taking over the ship."

"But, Father, I did not mean—"

The Bishop waved away her protestations. "Oh, I know you mean no harm, Sister. As I was saying, my thought was that it would be quite nice if you moved your shrine to the Holy Mother on deck, perhaps just above us, in the aft promenade that is nicely sheltered. Perhaps the crew would like to join in your daily devotions." He bowed to the Commodore and added, "As time and their duties would allow, of course."

"Of course—of course," parroted the Commodore.

"Well, certainly I could do that. As long as the weather remains clear," said Marie Madeleine.

"Thank you, Sister. Consider it a personal favor to me."

"Very well, then. I feel we have accomplished so much tonight," the nun said enthusiastically. "*Au revoir, monsieurs. Allons-y, mademoiselles,*" she concluded, and then herded her group from the room.

Lenobia felt the Bishop's gaze until the door closed, blocking his view of her.

"Well, then, shall we walk a little?" Without waiting for a response, Marie Madeleine strode purposefully to the short stairwell that led to the deck, where she breathed deeply and encouraged the girls to "walk about—stretch your young legs."

As Lenobia passed the nun, she asked softly, "What could he possibly want with the Holy Mother?"

"I have no idea," Marie Madeleine said. "But it certainly cannot hurt the Blessed Virgin to take a turn above deck." She paused, smiled at Lenobia, and added, "Just as it will not hurt the rest of us."

"For what you did tonight, Sister, *merci beaucoup.*"

"You are quite welcome, Lenobia."

The Bishop made his excuses and left the Commodore to his port. He retired to his small bedchamber, sat at the single desk, and lit one long, thin candlestick. As his fingers caressed the flame, he thought about the bastard girl.

At first he had been enraged and shocked by her deception. But then as he watched her, his rage and surprise coalesced to form a much deeper emotion.

Charles had forgotten the girl's beauty, though the many weeks of forced celibacy aboard this accursed ship could have something to do with her effect upon him.

"No," he spoke to the flame. "It is more than my lack of a bedmate that makes her desirable."

She was even lovelier than he'd remembered, though she had lost weight. That was a shame, but easily remedied. He liked her softer, rounder, more succulent. He would make sure she ate—whether she wanted to or not.

"No," he repeated. "There *is* more to it." It was those eyes. That hair. The eyes smoldered, like smoke. He could see that they called to him, even though she was trying to deny their pull.

The hair was silver, like metal that had been tested and hardened by fire, and then pounded into something more than it had once been.

"And she is not a true *fille à la casquette*. She will never be the bride of a French gentleman. She is, in fact, fortunate to have caught my attention. Being my mistress is more, much more than she has to hope for from her future."

Ridicule and disdain are less offensive than the Bishop's attention. The memory of her words came to him, but he did not allow himself to become angry.

"She will take convincing. No matter. I like it better if they have some spirit."

His fingers passed through the flame, over and over, absorbing heat but not burning.

It would be good to make the girl his mistress before they reached New Orleans. Then those pompous Ursulines would have nothing about which to squawk. A virgin girl they might care about—a deflowered bastard who had become the mistress of a Bishop would be out of their care and beyond their reach.

But first he must make her his own, and in order to do that he needed to silence that Virgin-be-damned nun.

His free hand fisted around the ruby cross that hung in the middle of his chest and the flame flickered wildly.

It was only the nun's protection that was keeping the bastard from being his plaything for the rest of the journey and beyond—only the nun who could draw down the wrath of the church upon him. The other girls were inconsequential. They would not consider standing against him, much less speaking against him to any authority. The

Commodore cared for nothing except a smooth voyage and his wine. As long as Charles did not rape her in front of the man, he would probably show only a mild interest, though possibly he might want to use the girl himself.

The Bishop's hand, the one that had been stroking the flame, closed in a fist. He did not share his possessions.

"Yes, I will have to rid myself of the nun." Charles smiled and relaxed his hand, allowing it to play through the flame again. "And I have already taken steps to hasten her untimely end. It is such a shame that the habit she wears is so voluminous and so highly flammable. I can sense a terrible accident might befall her . . ."

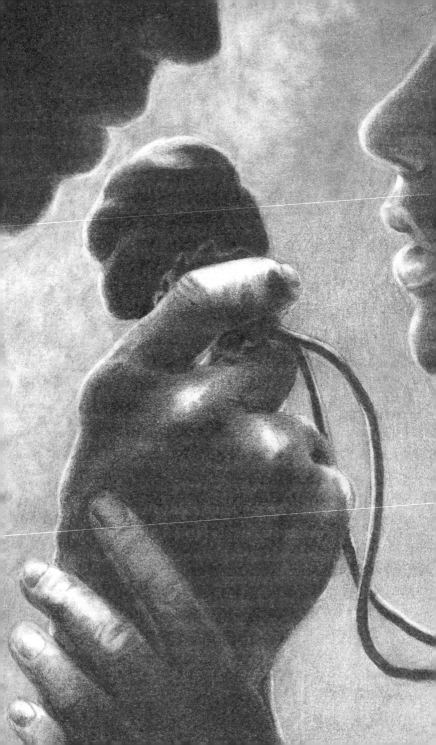

CHAPTER SIX

Dawn could not come soon enough for Lenobia. Finally, when the sky through her porthole began to blush, Lenobia could wait no longer. She almost sprinted to the door, pausing only because Marie Madeleine's voice warned, "Have a care, child. Do not remain too long with the horses. Staying out of the Bishop's sight means you are staying out of his mind as well."

"I will be careful, Sister," Lenobia assured her before disappearing into the hallway. She did watch for the sunrise, though her thoughts were already belowdecks, and before the orange disc had fully broken free of the watery horizon, Lenobia was hurrying silently but quickly down the stairs.

Martin was already there, sitting on a bale of hay, facing the direction from which she usually came into the cargo hold. The grays whinnied at her, which made her smile, and then she looked at Martin, and her smile faded.

The first thing she noticed was that he hadn't brought

her a bacon and cheese sandwich. The next thing she noticed was the absence of expression on his face. Even his eyes seemed darker and subdued. Suddenly he was a stranger.

"What do I call you?" His voice was as emotionless as his face.

She ignored his strangeness and the awful feeling it gave her in the pit of her stomach, and spoke to him as if he were asking her which brush to use on the horses, like nothing at all was amiss. "Lenobia is my name, but I like it when you call me *cherie*."

"You lie to me, you." His tone stopped her pretense and she felt the first chill of rejection pass through her body.

"Not on purpose. I did not lie to you on purpose." Her eyes begged him to understand.

"A lie still a lie," he said.

"All right. You want to know the truth?"

"Can you tell it?"

She felt as if he had slapped her. "I thought you knew me."

"I thought I did, too. And I thought you trusted me. Maybe I was wrong twice."

"I do trust you. The reason I did not tell you I was pretending to be Cecile was because when I was with you, I was the real me. There was no pretense between us. There was just you and me and the horses." She blinked back her tears and took a few steps toward him. "I would not lie to you, Martin. Yesterday was the first time you called me by her name, called me Cecile. Remember how quickly I left?" He nodded. "It was because I did not know what to do. It was then that I remembered I was supposed to be pretending to be someone else, even with you." There was a long silence, and then he asked, "Would you have ever told me?"

Lenobia didn't hesitate. She spoke from her heart to his. "Yes. I would have told you my secret when I told you I loved you."

His face reanimated and he closed the few feet that separated them. "No, *cherie*. You cannot love me."

"Cannot? I already do."

"It is impossible." Martin reached out, took her hand, and lifted it gently. Then he raised his own arm until the two were side by side, flesh to flesh. "You see the difference, you?"

"No," she said softly, gazing down at their arms—their bodies. "All I see is you."

"Look with your eyes and not your heart. See what others will see!"

"Others? Why do we care what they will see?"

"The world matters, perhaps more than you understand, *cherie*."

She met his gaze. "So you care more for what others think than for what we feel, you and I?"

"You do not understand."

"I understand enough! I understand how I feel when we are together. What more is there to understand?"

"Much, much more." He dropped her hand and turned, walking quickly to the stall to stand beside one of the watching grays.

She spoke to his back. "I said I would not lie to you. Can you say the same to me?"

"I will not lie to you," he said, without turning to look at her.

"Do you love me? Tell me the truth, Martin, please."

"The truth? What difference does the truth make in a world like this?"

"It makes all the difference to me," she said.

He turned and she saw that his cheeks were wet with silent tears. "I love you, *cherie*. It feels like it will kill me, but I love you."

Her heart felt as if it were flying as she moved to his side and slipped her hand within his. "I am no longer betrothed to Thinton de Silegne," she said, reaching up to brush the tears from his face.

He cupped his hand over hers and pressed it to his cheek. "But they will find someone new for you. Someone who cares more about your beauty than your name." As he spoke he grimaced as if the words hurt him.

"You! Why can it not be you? I am a bastard—surely a bastard can marry a Creole."

Martin laughed humorously. "*Oui, cherie*. A bastard can marry a Creole, if that bastard be black. If she be white, they cannot marry."

"Then I do not care about being married! I only care about being with you."

"You are so young," he said softly.

"So are you. You cannot be twenty yet."

"I be twenty-one next month, *cherie*. But inside I am old, and I know even love can not change the world—at least not in time for us."

"It has to. I am going to make it."

"You know what they do to you, this world you think love can change? They find out you love me, you give yourself to me, they hang you, or worse. They rape you and then hang you."

"I will fight them. To be with you I will stand against the world."

"I don' want that for you! *Cherie*, I will not be the cause of harm to come against you!"

Lenobia stepped back, away from his touch. "My maman told me that I must be brave. I must become a girl who was dead so that I could live a life without fear. So I did that terrible thing I did not want to do—I lied and tried to take on the name, the life, of someone else." As she spoke, it was as if a wise mother were whispering to her, guiding her thoughts and her words. "I was afraid, so afraid, Martin. But I knew I had to be brave for her, and then somehow that changed and I became brave for me. Now I want to be brave for you, for us."

"That not brave, *cherie*," he said, his olive eyes sad, his shoulders slumped. "That just young. You and me—our love belong to a different time, a different place."

"Then you deny us?"

"My heart cannot, but my mind—he say keep her safe, don' let the world destroy her." He took a step toward her, but Lenobia wrapped her arms around herself and stepped back from him. He shook his head sadly. "You should have babies, *cherie*. Babies that don' have to pretend to be white. I think you know a little what it like to pretend, don't you?"

"Here is what I know—that I would rather pretend a thousand times over than deny my love for you. Yes, I am young, but I am old enough to know that one-sided love can never work." When he said nothing, she wiped the back of her wrist angrily across her face, sweeping away her tears, and continued, "I should leave and not come back and spend the rest of the voyage anywhere but down here."

"*Oui, cherie*. You should."

"Is that what you want?"

"No, fool that I am. It is not what I want."

"Well, then, we are both fools." She walked past him and picked up one of the curry brushes. "I am going to groom the grays. Then I will feed them. Then I will return to my quarters and wait until tomorrow's dawn calls me free. Then I will do the same thing all over again." She moved into the stall and began brushing the nearest gray.

Still outside the stall, he watched her with olive eyes that she thought looked sad and very, very old. "You are brave, Lenobia. And strong. And good. When you are a woman grown, you will stand against the darkness in the world. I know this when I look into your storm-cloud eyes. But, *ma belle,* choose battles you can win without losing your heart and your soul."

"Martin, I stopped being a girl when I stepped into Cecile's shoes. I am a woman grown. I wish you understood that."

He sighed and nodded. "You right. I know you a woman, but I not the only one who knows this. *Cherie,* I heard talk today from the Commodore's servants. That Bishop, he don' keep his eyes from you all during dinner."

"Sister Marie Madeleine and I have already spoken of it. I am going to stay out of his sight as much as possible."

She met his gaze. "You do not need to worry about me. I have been avoiding the Bishop and men like him for the past two years."

"From what I see, there are not many men like the Bishop. I feel something bad follows him. His bakas, I think it turn against him."

"Bakas? What is that?" Lenobia paused in grooming the gray and leaned against the big horse's side while Martin explained.

"Think of a bakas like a soul catcher, and it catch two kind of souls—high and low. Balance is best for a bakas. We all have good and bad in us, *cherie*. But if the wearer is out of balance—if he do evil, then the bakas turn against him and there is darkness set free, terrible to behold."

"How do you know all of this?"

"My maman, she come from Haiti, along with many of my father's slaves. It the old religion that they follow. They raised me. I follow it." He shrugged and smiled at her wide-eyed expression. "I think we all come from the same place—we all go back there someday, too. Just lots of different names for that place because there are so many different kinds of people."

"But the Bishop is a Catholic priest. How could he know about an old religion from Haiti?"

"*Cherie*, you don' have to be told about a thing to feel

it—to know it. Bakas are real, and sometimes they find the wearer. That ruby he wear around his neck—that a bakas if I ever see one."

"The ruby is a cross, Martin."

"It also a bakas, and one that has turned to bad, *cherie*."

Lenobia shivered. "He frightens me, Martin. He always has."

Martin strode over to her and reached under his shirt, pulling out a long piece of slender leather tied to a small leather pouch that had been dyed a beautiful sapphire blue. He pulled it from around his neck and put it around hers. "This gris-gris protect you, *cherie*."

Lenobia fingered the little pouch. "What is in it?"

"I wear it 'most my whole life and I don' know for certain. I know there thirteen small things in it. Before she die, my maman she make it for me to protect me. It worked for me." Martin took the pouch from her fingers. Looking deeply in her eyes, he raised it to his lips and kissed it. "Now it work for you." Then slowly, deliberately, he hooked one finger on the fabric in the front of her bodice and pulled gently so that the shift came away from her skin. He dropped the little bag within, where it lay against her breast, just above her mother's rosary. "Wear it close to your heart, *cherie,* and the power of my maman's people will never be far from you."

His nearness made it hard for her to breathe and when he released her, Lenobia thought she felt the warmth of his kiss through the little jewel-colored pouch.

"If you give me your mother's protection, then I have to replace it with my mother's." She took the rosary beads from around her neck and held them out to him.

He smiled and bent so she could put them on him. He lifted a bead and studied it. "Carved wooden roses. You know what my maman's people use rose oil for, *cherie*?"

"No." She still felt breathless at his closeness and at the intensity of his gaze.

"Rose oil make potent love spells," he said, the corners of his lips lifting. "You trying to bespell me, *cherie*?"

"Maybe," Lenobia said, their gazes locking and holding.

Then the gelding butted her playfully and stamped one large hoof, impatient that his grooming hadn't been completed.

Martin's laugh broke the tension that had been building between them. "I think I have competition for your favors. The grays, they not share you."

"Jealous boy," Lenobia murmured, turning to hug the gelding's wide neck and retrieve the curry brush from the sawdust on the ground.

Still chuckling softly, Martin fetched the wide, wooden comb and got to work on the other gray's mane and tail.

"What story for you today, *cherie*?"

"Tell me about the horses on your father's plantation," she said. "You started to a few days ago and never finished."

While Martin talked about Rillieux's specialty, a new breed of horse that could run a quarter mile with such speed they were being compared to winged Pegasus, Lenobia let her mind wander. *We have two more weeks left in the voyage. He already loves me.* She pressed her hand against her breast, feeling the warmth of his mother's gris-gris. *If we stand together, we'll be brave enough to stand against the world.*

Lenobia felt hopeful and so very alive as she climbed the stairs from the cargo hold to the hallway that led to her quarters. Martin had filled her head with stories of his father's amazing horses, and somewhere in the middle of his tales she'd had a wonderful idea: perhaps she and Martin could stay in New Orleans only as long as it took to earn enough money to purchase a young stallion from Rillieux. Then they could take their wingless Pegasus and go west with him and find a place where they wouldn't be judged by the color of their skin, and could settle down and breed beautiful, swift horses. *And children,* her thoughts whispered to her, *lots of beautiful brown-skinned children just like Martin.*

She would ask Marie Madeleine to help her find employment, maybe even something in the Ursuline nuns' kitchen. Everyone needed a scullery maid who could bake delicious bread—and Lenobia had learned that skill from the Baron's host of talented French chefs.

"Your smile makes you even more lovely, Lenobia."

She hadn't heard him enter the hallway, but he was suddenly there, blocking her way. Lenobia's hand went up to touch the leather thong hidden under her chemise. She thought about Martin and the power of his mother's protection, raised her chin, and met the Bishop's gaze.

"*Excusez moi,* Father," she said coldly. "I must get back to Sister Marie Madeleine. She will be at her morning prayers, and I would very much like to join her."

"Surely you are not angry with me about yesterday. You

must realize what a shock it was to realize your deception."
As the Bishop spoke, he stroked the ruby cross. Lenobia
watched him carefully, thinking how odd it was that it
seemed to flash and shine even in the dim light of the pas-
sageway.

"I would not dare to be angry with you, Father. I only
wish to return to our good Sister."

He stepped closer to her. "I have a proposal for you, and
when you hear it you will know that with the great honor
I pay you, you can dare much more than anger."

"I am sorry, Father. I do not know what you could mean,"
she said, trying to sidle around him.

"Do you not, *ma petite de bas*? I look in those eyes of
yours and I see many things."

Lenobia's anger at what he was calling her overrode her
fear. "My name is Lenobia Whitehall. I am not your bastard!" She hurled the words at him.

His smile was terrible. Suddenly his arms snaked out,
one hand on either side of Lenobia, pinning her against
the wall. The sleeves of his purple robe were like curtains,
veiling her from the real world. He was so tall that the ruby
crucifix dangled in front of her eyes and for a moment she
thought she saw flames within its glistening depths.

Then he spoke, and her world narrowed to the stench
of his breath and the heat of his body.

"When I am finished with you, you will be anything I desire you to be—bastard, whore, lover, daughter. Anything. But do not give in too easily, *ma petite de bas*. I like a struggle."

"Father, there you are! How fortuitous that I should find you so close to our quarters. Could you please help me? I thought moving the Holy Mother would be simply done, but I either underestimated her weight or overestimated my strength."

The Bishop stepped back, releasing Lenobia. She sprinted down the hallway to the nun, who was not looking at them at all. Instead she was struggling to drag a large painted stone statue of Mary from the doorway of their room out into the hall. As Lenobia reached her, the nun glanced up and said, "Lenobia, good. Please get the altar candle and the incense brazier. We will be saying the Marian litanies, as well as the Little Office of the Virgin, on deck today and for the next few days until we reach port in New Orleans."

"Few days? You are mistaken, Sister," the Bishop said condescendingly. "We have at least two more weeks remaining in our voyage."

Marie Madeleine straightened from wrestling with the statue and rubbed the small of her back as she gave the Bishop a cold look that completely belied her offhanded manner and the coincidence of interrupting his abuse of

Lenobia. "Days," she said sternly. "I just spoke to the Commodore. The squall put us ahead of schedule. We will be in New Orleans in three or four days. It will be lovely for us all to be on land again, will it not? I will be especially pleased to introduce you to our Mother Superior and tell her what a safe and pleasant voyage we all have had thanks to your protection. You do know how well she is thought of in the city, do you not, Bishop de Beaumont?"

There was a long silence and then the Bishop said, "Oh, yes, Sister. I know that and much, much more."

Then the priest bent and lifted the heavy statue as if it were made of feathers rather than stone, and carried it above deck.

"Did he harm you?" Marie Madeleine whispered quickly as soon as he was out of sight.

"No," Lenobia said shakily. "But he wants to."

The nun nodded grimly. "Get the candle and incense. Wake the other girls and tell them to come up for prayers. Then stay close to me. You will have to forgo your solitary dawn trips. It simply is not safe. Thankfully, we only have a few short days. Then you will be at the convent and beyond his reach." The nun squeezed her hand before following the Bishop to the upper deck, leaving Lenobia alone and utterly brokenhearted.

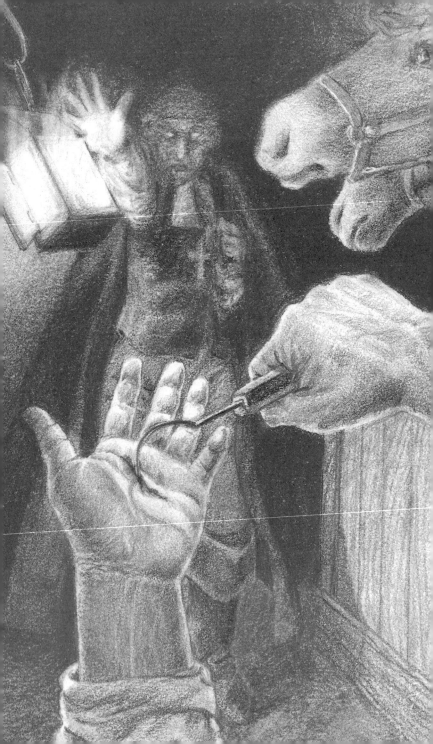

CHAPTER SEVEN

Later, when her world had turned dark and painful and filled with despair, Lenobia remembered that morning and the beauty of the sky and the sea—and how everything had changed so suddenly and completely in less than the time it took her heart to beat a dozen times. She remembered it, and vowed that for the rest of her life she would not take anything beautiful and special for granted

It had been early, and the girls had been sluggish and peevish, not wanting to rise. Not wanting to go up on deck to pray. Aveline de Lafayette was especially annoyed, though Simonette's excitement about something new more than made up for the older girl's sour disposition.

"I have so wanted to explore the ship," Simonette confided in Lenobia as they made their way to the little promenade area in the aft of the *Minerva*.

"It is a very beautiful ship," Lenobia murmured back, and then smiled as Simonette's curls bounced and bobbed as she nodded her head in response.

The marble statue of Mary had been placed near the black railing that framed the aft portion of the ship—sitting just above the Commodore's own quarters. Sister Marie Madeleine was fussing with the statue, scooting it around and placing it just right, until she saw Lenobia, and then she motioned for the girl to come to her.

"Child, I will take the taper and the incense."

Lenobia gave her the silver incense burner, which was already filled with the precious mixture of frankincense and myrrh the nun used when she was at prayer, as well as the thick beeswax pillar resting in its plain pewter holder. She returned to the statue and placed the candle and the incense burner at Mary's feet.

"Girls," the nun addressed her crowd, and then with a slight smile she nodded her head in acknowledgment of the crew members who were beginning to congregate curiously toward them. "And good gentlemen. Let us begin this lovely morning with the Marian litanies as a thanksgiving for the news that we are mere days from our destination of New Orleans." She motioned for the watching crew to come closer.

As they approached, Lenobia looked for Martin in the group but was disappointed when she did not see his familiar face.

"Oh, my! We need a brand from below to light Mary's taper. Lenobia, child, could you please—"

"Do not fret, Sister. I will light Mary's fire."

The girls parted like fog to sunlight and the Bishop strode through them with a long wooden brand in his hand, the end of which flickered with flame. He offered it to the nun, and she took it with a strained smile.

"Thank you, Father. Would you like to lead the Marian litany this morning?"

"No, Sister. I believe the litanies of Mary are more fully appreciated when led by a woman." With a bow of his head, the Bishop retreated to the far side of the aft promenade, where the crew members were gathering. He stood in front of them.

Lenobia thought his choice of position made it appear uncomfortably as if he were planning to lead the phalanx of men against them.

Nonplussed, Sister Marie Madeleine lit the candle and the incense. Then she knelt and genuflected. Lenobia and the rest of the girls followed her example. Lenobia was positioned to the nun's left, facing the statue, but also turned so that she could see the Bishop—so she saw his arrogant hesitation, which made his kneeling appear patronizing rather than obedient. The men around him followed suit.

Marie Madeleine bowed her head and pressed her hands together prayerfully. With closed eyes she began the litany in a clear, strong voice:

"Holy Mary, pray for us."

"Pray for us," the girls repeated obediently.

"Holy Mother of God," Marie Madeleine intoned.

"Pray for us." This time the crew members took up the litany and added their voices to the prayer.

"Holy Virgin of virgins."

"Pray for us," the crowd invoked.

"Mother of Christ," the nun continued.

"Pray for us . . ."

Lenobia repeated the phrase, but she was unable to quiet her spirit enough to close her eyes and bow her head, as were the other girls. Instead her gaze and her mind wandered.

"Pray for us . . ."

Three days left in the voyage, and Marie Madeleine says I cannot go to the cargo hold again.

"Mother of divine grace."

"Pray for us . . ."

Martin! How am I going to get word to him? I must see him again, even if it means I chance another encounter with the Bishop.

"Mother most pure."

"Pray for us . . ."

Lenobia's gaze flitted to the group of men and the man in purple robes who knelt before them. Her eyes widened in shock. He did not have his head bowed and his eyes closed. He was staring at the statue, in front of which the nun was on her knees in prayer. His hands were not folded. Instead, one hand was stroking the shining ruby crucifix that hung in the middle of his chest. The other was making a slight but odd motion, just a flutter of his fingers, almost as if he were beckoning movement from something before him.

"Mother most chaste."

"Pray for us . . ."

Confused, Lenobia followed the Bishop's gaze and realized the priest was staring not at the statue but at the single thick pillar candle lit at the feet of Mary, directly in front of the nun. It was at that moment that the flame intensified, blazing with such a fierce intensity that wax seemed to weep from it. Then wax and flame joined as sparks, and fire exploded from the taper and cascaded onto Marie Madeleine's linen habit.

"Sister! The fire!" Lenobia cried, getting to her feet to run toward Marie Madeleine.

But the strange fire had already become a terrible blaze. The nun cried out and tried to stand, but she was obviously disoriented by the flames that were consuming her. Instead of moving away from the wildly burning pillar, Marie Madeleine lurched forward, directly into the pool of burning wax.

Girls all around Lenobia were screaming and bumping into her, keeping her from reaching the nun.

"Get back! I will save her!" the Bishop yelled as he ran forward, purple robes billowing like flame behind him, with a bucket in his hands.

"No!" Lenobia screamed, remembering the lessons she had learned in the kitchen about wax and grease and water. "Get a blanket, not water! Smother it!"

The Bishop threw the bucket of water on the burning nun, and the fire exploded, raining flaming hot wax into the crowd of girls and creating panic and hysteria.

The world became fire and heat. Still, Lenobia tried to get to Marie Madeleine, but strong hands entrapped her waist and pulled her back.

"No!" she screamed, fighting to get away.

"*Cherie!* You cannot help her!"

Martin's voice was an oasis of calm in chaos, and Lenobia's body went limp. She let him pull her back out of range of the burning aft deck. But in the midst of the flames Lenobia saw Marie Madeleine stop struggling. Completely engulfed in flame, the nun walked to the railing, turned, and for an instant her gaze met Lenobia's.

Lenobia would never forget that moment. What she saw in Marie Madeleine's eyes was not pain or terror or fear. She saw peace. And within her mind echoed the nun's voice, mixed with another that was stronger, clearer, and otherworldly in its beauty. *Follow your heart, child. The Mother shall always protect you . . .*

Then the nun stepped over the railing and purposely leaped overboard into the cool, welcoming arms of the sea.

The next thing Lenobia remembered was Martin ripping off his shirt and using it to beat out the flames that had been licking at her skirt.

"You stay here!" he shouted at her when the fire was out. "Don' move, you!" Lenobia nodded woodenly, and then Martin joined the other crew members as they used clothes and pieces of sails and rigging to pound out the fire. Commodore Cornwallis was there, shouting orders and using his blue dress jacket to beat out pockets of fire, which now seemed to extinguish with an unnatural ease.

"I was trying to help! I did not know!" Lenobia's gaze was drawn by the Bishop's cries. He was standing at the railing, looking over into the sea.

"Charles! Are you burned? Are you injured?" Lenobia watched the Commodore hurry over to him just as the priest swayed and almost fell overboard. The Commodore caught him in time. "Come away from the railing, man!"

"No, no." The Bishop shook him off. "I must do this. I

must." He lifted his arm, made the sign of the cross, and then Lenobia heard him begin the last rites prayer. *"Domine sancte . . ."*

Lenobia had never loathed anyone so much in her life.

Simonette lurched into her arms, pink and singed and sobbing. "What do we do now? What do we do now?"

Lenobia clung to Simonette, but she could not answer the girl.

"Mademoiselles! Are any of you injured?" The Commodore's voice boomed as he waded through the group of weeping girls, pulling out those who had been closest to the flames and directing the ship's surgeon to them. "If you are uninjured, go below. Clean yourselves. Change your clothes. Rest, mademoiselles, rest. The fire is out. The ship is sound. You are safe."

Martin was lost in the smoke and confusion, and Lenobia had no choice but to go below with Simonette still holding tightly to her hand.

"Did you hear her, too?" Lenobia whispered as they made their way, trembling and crying, down the narrow hallway.

"I heard the Sister scream. It was terrible." Simonette sobbed.

"Nothing else? You did not hear what she said?" Lenobia persisted.

"She said nothing. She only screamed." Simonette gazed

at her with wide, tear-filled eyes. "Have you gone mad, Lenobia?"

"No, no," Lenobia said quickly, putting a reassuring arm around her shoulders. "I almost wish I was mad, though, so I would not have to remember what just happened."

Simonette sobbed anew. "*Oui, oui*—I will not leave the room until we have reached land. Not even to go to dinner. They cannot force me!"

Lenobia hugged her tightly and said nothing more.

Lenobia did not leave her quarters for the next two days. Simonette needn't have worried about being forced to the Commodore's room for the evening meals. Food was brought to them instead. Sister Marie Madeleine's death had cast a spell over them all, and the normal fabric of shipboard life had unraveled. The loud and sometimes bawdy songs the crew had been singing for weeks were no more. There was no laughter. No shouting. The ship itself seemed to have gone silent. Within hours of the nun's death a fierce wind came up from behind them, caught the sails, and propelled them forward as if the breath of God were blowing them from the site of violence.

In their quarters, the girls were in shock. Simonette and a few others still wept on and off. Mostly they huddled on their pallets, talked in hushed voices, or prayed.

The galley servants who brought them food assured them all was well and that they would make land soon. The pronouncement evoked nothing but somber looks and silent tears.

All the while Lenobia thought and remembered.

She remembered Marie Madeleine's kindness. She remembered the nun's faith and strength. She remembered the peace she'd seen in her dying eyes and the words that had echoed magickally through her mind.

Follow your heart, child. The Mother shall always protect you.

Lenobia remembered Sister Marie Madeleine, but she thought about Martin. She also thought about the future. It was just before dawn of the third day that Lenobia made her decision, and she crept silently from the room that had begun to feel like a mausoleum.

She did not watch the dawn. She went directly to the cargo hold. Odysseus, the black and white giant of a cat, was rubbing against her legs as she got close to the stall. The horses saw her first, and both grays trumpeted greetings, which had Martin whirling around, closing the space between them in three long strides, and pulling her into his arms, hugging her close. She could feel his body trembling as he spoke.

"You came, *cherie*! I don' think you would. I think I never see you again."

Lenobia rested her head against his chest and breathed in the scent of him: horses, hay, and the honest sweat of a man who worked hard every day.

"I had to think before I came to see you, Martin. I had to decide."

"What is it you decide, *cherie*?"

She lifted her head and looked up at him, loving the light olive of his eyes and the brown flecks that sparkled like amber within them. "First, I have to ask you something—did you see her jump into the ocean?"

Martin nodded solemnly. "I did, *cherie*. It was a terrible thing."

"Did you hear anything?"

"Only her screams."

Lenobia drew a deep breath. "Just before she leaped

overboard she looked at me, Martin. Her eyes were full of peace, not fear or pain. And I did not hear her screams. Instead I heard her voice, mixed with another's, telling me to follow my heart—that the Mother shall always protect me."

"The nun, she was a very holy woman—one of much faith and goodness. Her spirit strong. It might have been speaking to you. Maybe her Mary she love so much speaking to you, too."

Lenobia felt weak with relief. "Then you believe me!"

"*Oui, cherie*. I know there more to the world than what we can see and touch."

"I believe that, too." She drew a deep breath and squared her shoulders and, in a voice that surprised even herself by how grown-up she sounded, she declared, "At least now I do. So what I want to say to you is this: I love you, Martin, and I want to be with you. Always. I do not care how. I do not care where. But seeing Marie Madeleine die has changed me. If the worst that can happen to me for choosing to live by your side is that I die in peace loving you, then I choose whatever happiness we can find in this world."

"*Cherie*, I—"

"No. Do not answer me now. Take two days after we dock, just like I took two days. You have to know for sure either way, Martin. If you say no, then I do not want to see you again—ever. If you choose yes, I will live by your side and bear your children. I will love you until the day I die—only you, Martin. Always only you; I vow it."

Then, before she could weaken and beg him and hold him and weep, she walked away from him and picked up the familiar curry brush and entered the Percherons' stall, caressing the big horses and murmuring endearments in greeting.

Martin followed her slowly. Not speaking to her or looking at her, he moved to the second of the two geldings and began working his way through the tangle of the horse's mane. Thus he was hidden from the Bishop's view when the priest entered the cargo hold.

"Grooming beasts—not a job for a lady. But then you are no lady are you, *ma petite de bas*?"

Lenobia felt sickness slick through her stomach, but she turned to face the priest whom she thought of as more monster than man.

"I told you not to call me that," Lenobia said, proud that her voice did not shake.

"And I told you I like a fight." His smile was reptilian. "But fight or no fight, when I am finished with you, you will be anything I desire you to be—bastard, whore, lover, daughter. Anything." He moved forward, the light in the ruby cross on his chest glowing as if it were a living thing.

"Who will protect you now that your shielding nun has been consumed?" He reached the edge of the stall, and Lenobia cringed, pressing herself against the gelding. "Time is short, *ma petite de bas*. I will claim you as mine today, before we get to New Orleans, and then there will be no reason for you to keep up this virginal charade and cower with the Ursulines in their convent." The priest put his hand on the half door of the stall to open it.

Martin stepped from the shadow of the horses to stand between Lenobia and the Bishop. He spoke calmly, but he was brandishing a hoof pick in his hand. The lantern light caught it and it glistened, knifelike.

"I think you not be claiming this lady. She don' want you, Loa. Go now, and leave her be."

The Bishop's eyes narrowed dangerously and his fingers began to stroke the ruby stones of his crucifix. "You dare speak to me, boy? You should understand who I am. I am not this loa you have mistaken me for. I am a Bishop—a man of God. Leave now and I will forget you ever attempted to question me."

"Loa is spirit. I see you. I know you. The bakas has turned on you, man. You evil. You dark. And you not wanted here."

"You dare stand against me!" the priest roared. As his anger grew, so too did the flames in the lanterns that hung around the stalls.

"Martin! The flames!" Lenobia whispered frantically to him.

The priest began to move forward, as if he would attack Martin with his bare hands, and two things happened very quickly. First, Martin lifted the hoof pick, but he didn't strike the priest. Instead he wielded it against himself. Lenobia gasped as Martin slashed his own palm and then, as the priest was almost on him, he flung the handful of blood at him, striking him in the middle of his chest, covering the red jewels with living scarlet. And in a voice that was deep and filled with power, Martin intoned:

> *"She belong to me—and hers I be!*
> *"Of loyalty and truth,*
> *"This blood be my proof!*
> *"What you do to her you do in vain.*
> *"What you cast come back on you tenfold the pain!"*

The priest staggered to the side, as if the blood had been a blow, and the geldings laid their ears back flat on their enormous heads and, with squeals of rage, struck out at him with their great, square teeth.

Charles de Beaumont lurched back, stumbling out of the stall, clutching his chest. He bent over and stared at Martin.

Martin raised his bloody hand and held it, palm out, like a shield.

"You asked who protect this girl? I answer you—I do. The spell is cast. I seal it with my blood. You don' have no power here."

The priest's eyes were filled with hatred, his voice malicious. "Your blood spell may lend you power here, but you will not have power where we are going. There you are only a black man trying to stand against a white man. I will win . . . I will win . . . I will win . . ." The Bishop muttered the words over and over as he left the cargo hold, still clutching his chest.

As soon as he was gone, Martin pulled Lenobia into his arms and held her while she trembled. He stroked her hair and murmured small, wordless sounds to soothe her. When her fear had ebbed enough, Lenobia moved from his arms and ripped a strip of cotton from her chemise to bind his hand. She didn't speak while she was bandaging him. It was only when she was finished that she clasped his wounded hand within both of hers and looked up into his eyes asking, "That thing you said—that spell you cast—is it true? Will it really work?"

"Oh, it work, *cherie,*" he said. "Work enough to keep him from you on this ship. But this man, he filled with great evil. You know he cause the fire that killed the holy woman?"

Lenobia nodded. "Yes, I know it."

"His bakas—it strong; it evil. I bind him with tenfold pain, but come a time maybe when he think having you worth the pain. And he right. In the world we go to he have the power, not me."

"But you stopped him!"

Martin nodded. "I can fight him with my maman's magick, but I don' fight white men and their law he can bring against me."

"Then you have to leave New Orleans. Get far away, where he cannot hurt you."

Martin smiled. *"Oui, cherie, avec tu."*

"With me?" Lenobia stared at him for a moment, worry for him foremost in her mind. Then she realized what he had said and she felt as if the dawn had risen within her. "With me! We will be together."

Martin pulled her into his arms again and held her close. "It is what made my magick so strong, *cherie*, this love I have for you. It fills my blood and makes my heart to beat. Now my vow you have in return. I will always love you—only you, Lenobia."

Lenobia pressed her face to his chest and this time when she wept, her tears were of happiness.

CHAPTER EIGHT

It was that evening, March 21, 1788, as the sun was an orange globe settling into the water, that the *Minerva* sailed into the port of New Orleans.

It was also that evening that Lenobia began to cough.

She started feeling ill just after she returned to her quarters. At first she thought it was that she hated leaving Martin, and that the room that had seemed a sanctuary when Sister Marie Madeleine had been there now felt more like a prison. Lenobia could not make herself eat breakfast. By the time the excited shout of "Land! I see land!" was ringing across the ship and the girls were hesitantly emerging from their rooms to huddle together on the deck, staring at the growing mass of land before them, Lenobia was feeling flushed and had to muffle her coughs in her sleeve.

"Mademoiselles, I would not usually have you disembark in darkness, but because of the recent tragedy with Sister Marie Madeleine, I believe it is best that you are landed and safely within the Ursuline convent as soon as is possible." The Commodore made the pronouncement to the girls on deck. "I know the Abbess. I will go to her immediately and tell her of the loss of the Sister, and announce to her that you will be coming ashore tonight. Please take only your small *casquettes* with you. I will have the rest of your things delivered to the convent." He bowed and headed to the side of the deck from which the rowboat would be lowered.

In her feverish state, it seemed her mother's voice returned to Lenobia, admonishing her not to call it a word that sounded so much like casket. Lenobia moved slowly belowdecks with the rest of the girls, feeling eerily like the voice from the past was an omen of the future.

No! She shook off the melancholy she was feeling. *I have a slight ague. I will think of Martin. He is making plans for us to leave New Orleans and go west, where we will be together—forever.*

It was that thought that propelled her forward as she settled, shivering and coughing, in the small boat with the other girls. Once she was seated between Simonette and Colette, a young girl with long, dark hair, Lenobia looked around listlessly, trying to summon the energy to complete her journey. Her gaze passed over the rowers and olive eyes caught hers, telegraphing strength and love.

She must have made a sound of happy surprise, because Simonette asked, "What is it, Lenobia?"

Feeling renewed, Lenobia smiled at the girl. "I am happy that our long voyage is over, and eager to begin the next chapter of my life."

"You sound so certain it will be good," Simonette said.

"I am. I believe the next part of my life will be the very best," Lenobia responded, loud enough for her voice to carry to Martin.

The rowboat rocked as the last passenger joined them, saying, "I am quite certain it will be."

The strength she'd found in Martin's presence turned to fear and loathing as the Bishop settled into a seat so close to her that his purple robes, blowing in the warm, humid air, almost touched her skirts. There he sat, silent and staring.

Lenobia pulled her cloak closer to her and looked away, focusing on not allowing her gaze to turn to Martin while she ignored the Bishop. She breathed deeply of the muddy, earthy aroma of the port where river met sea, hoping the warm, moist air and the scent of land would soothe her cough.

It did not.

The Abbess, Sister Marie Therese, was a tall, thin woman who Lenobia thought looked oddly crowlike standing on the dock with her dark habit blowing around her. While the Commodore helped the Bishop exit the boat, the Abbess and two nuns who were pale faced and looked as though they had been weeping, helped the crew members pass the girls from the rowboat to the dock, saying, "Come, mademoiselles. You need rest and peace after the horror of what happened to our good Sister. Both await you at our convent."

When it was her turn to climb onto the dock, she felt the strength of familiar hands on hers, and he whispered, "Be brave, *ma cherie*. I will come for you." Lenobia's touch lingered in Martin's for as long as she dared, and then she took the nun's hand. She did not look back at Martin, but instead tried to muffle her cough and blend in with the group of girls.

When they were all onshore, the Abbess bowed her head slightly to the Bishop and the Commodore and said, "*Merci beaucoup* for delivering my charges unto me. I shall take them from here and will shortly place them safely into the hands of their husbands."

"Not all of them." The Bishop's voice was like a whip, but the Abbess hardly raised a brow at him when she responded. "Yes, Bishop, all of them. The Commodore has already explained to me the unfortunate mistake in the identity of one of the girls. That does not make her any less my charge—it simply changes the choice of husband for her."

Lenobia couldn't squelch the wet cough that racked her. The Bishop glanced sharply at her, but when he spoke his voice had taken on a smooth, charming tone. His expression was not angry or threatening—it was only concerned.

"I am afraid that the errant girl has become infected with something other than the sins of her mother. Do you truly want her contagion in your convent?"

The Abbess moved to stand beside Lenobia. She touched her face, lifting her chin and looking into her eyes. Lenobia tried to smile at her, but she simply felt too ill, too overwhelmed. And she was trying desperately and unsuccessfully not to cough. The nun smoothed back the silver hair from Lenobia's damp brow and murmured, "It has been a difficult journey for you, has it not, child?" Then she turned to face the Bishop. "And what would you have me do, Bishop? Not show her Christian charity at all and leave her on the dock?"

Lenobia watched his eyes flash with anger, but he tempered his rage, responding, "Of course not, Sister. Of course not. I am simply concerned for the greater good of the convent."

"That is quite considerate of you, Father. As the Commodore must return to his ship, perhaps you would show us further consideration by escorting our small group to the convent. I would like to say we are perfectly safe on the streets of our fair city, but that would not be entirely honest of me."

The Bishop bowed his head and smiled. "It would be a great honor for me to escort you."

"*Merci beaucoup*, Father," the Abbess said. She then motioned for the girls to follow her, saying, "Come, children, *allons-y*."

Lenobia moved away with the group, trying to keep to the middle of the pack of girls, though she felt the Bishop's eyes staying with her, following her, coveting her. She wanted to look for Martin, but was afraid to draw attention to him. As they walked away from the dock, she heard the sound of the rowboat's oars striking the water and knew he must be returning to the *Minerva*.

Please come for me soon, Martin! Please! Lenobia sent a silent plea into the night. And then she turned her entire concentration to putting one foot before the other and trying to breathe between coughing fits.

The walk to the convent took on a nightmare quality that eerily mirrored Lenobia's carriage ride from the château to Le Havre. There was no mist, but there was darkness and smells and sounds that were oddly familiar—French voices, beautiful filigreed ironwork galleries flanked by floating curtains through which crystal chandeliers twinkled—mixed with the strange sound of English spoken in a cadence that reminded her of Martin's musical accent. The foreign scents of spice and silty earth were tinged with the sweet, buttery aroma of fried beignets.

With each step, Lenobia felt herself getting weaker and weaker.

"Lenobia, come on—stay with us!"

Lenobia blinked through the sweat that had been running down her brow and into her eyes to see that Simonette had paused at the rear of the group to call to her.

How have I gotten so far behind them? Lenobia tried to hurry. Tried to catch up, but there was something in front of her—something small and furred that she stumbled over, almost falling to the cobblestoned street.

A strong, cool touch took her elbow, righting her, and Lenobia looked up into eyes blue as a spring sky and a face so beautiful she thought it otherworldly, especially as it was decorated with a tattoo pattern that was featherlike and intricate.

"My apology, daughter," the woman said, smiling an apology. "My cat often goes where he will. He has tripped up many who are healthier and stronger than you."

"I am stronger than I look," Lenobia heard herself rasping.

"It pleases me to hear you say so," the woman said before loosing Lenobia's elbow and walking away with a large gray tabby cat following her, tail twitching as if in irritation. As she passed the group of girls, she glanced at the head nun and bowed her head respectfully, saying, "*Bonsoir,* Abbess."

"*Bonsoir,* Priestess," the nun responded smoothly.

"That creature is a vampyre!" the Bishop exclaimed as the beautiful woman pulled up the hood of her black velvet cloak and faded into the shadows.

"*Oui,* indeed she is," said the Abbess.

Even through her illness Lenobia felt a start of surprise. She had heard of vampyres, of course, and knew there was a stronghold of them not far from Paris, but the village of Auvergne had none of them, nor had the Château de Navarre ever hosted a group of them, as some of the bolder, richer nobility occasionally did. Lenobia wished, fleetingly, that she had taken a longer look at the vampyre. Then the Bishop's voice intruded on her wishes.

"You suffer them to walk among you?"

The Abbess's serene look did not change. "There are many different types of people who come and go through New Orleans, Father. It is an entry point to a vast new world. You will become accustomed to our ways in due time. As to vampyres, I hear they are considering establishing a House of Night here."

"Certainly the city would not allow such a thing," the Bishop said.

"It is well known that where there is a House of Night, there is also beauty and civilization. That is something the fathers of this city would appreciate."

"You sound as if you approve."

"I approve of education. Each House of Night, at its heart, is a school."

"How do you know so much about vampyres, Abbess?" asked Simonette. Then she looked startled at her own question and added, "I do not mean disrespect by asking such a thing."

"Such a thing is normal curiosity," the Abbess responded with a kind smile. "My older sister was Marked and Changed to vampyre when I was just a child. She still visits my parents' home near Paris."

"Blasphemy," the Bishop muttered darkly.

"Some say so, some say so," the Abbess said, shrugging dismissively. Lenobia's next coughing spell pulled the nun's attention from the Bishop. "Child, I do not believe you are well enough to walk the rest of the way to the convent."

"I am sorry, Sister. I will be better if I rest for a moment."

Unexpectedly, at that moment Lenobia's legs became like water and she dropped to her bottom in the middle of the street.

"Father! Bring her here, quickly," the nun ordered.

Lenobia cringed at the Bishop's touch, but he only smiled and with one strong movement, bent and lifted her into his arms as if she were a child. Then he followed the nun into the long, narrow stables that connected two vividly painted homes, both with elaborate galleries that stretched the length of their second stories.

"Here, Father. She can rest comfortably on these bales of hay."

Lenobia felt the Bishop's hesitation, as if he did not want to let her go, but the Abbess repeated, "Father, here. This is where you may place her."

She was finally released from the cage of his arms, and she shrank back even farther, pulling her cloak with her so that nothing touched the priest, who lingered too close by.

Lenobia drew a deep breath and, as if by magick, the sound and scent of horses filled her and soothed her, relieving just a small amount of the burning in her chest.

"Child," the Abbess said, bending over her and brushing the hair from her brow again. "I am going to go on to the convent. Once there I will send our hospital carriage for you. Do not fear; it will not be long." She straightened and said to the priest, "Father, I would consider it a kindness if you remained with the child."

"No!" Lenobia shouted at the same moment the Bishop said, "*Oui,* of course."

The Abbess touched Lenobia's brow again and reassured her. "Child, I will return soon. The Bishop will watch over you until then."

"No, Sister. Please. I feel much better now. I can wal —" Lenobia's protestations were drowned in another fit of coughing.

The Abbess nodded sadly. "Yes, it is better if I send the carriage. I will return soon." She turned and hurried back to the street and the waiting girls, leaving Lenobia alone with the Bishop.

CHAPTER NINE

"There is no need for you to look so terrified. I find a struggling girl exciting, not a sick one." He peered into the stables as he spoke to her, though he didn't walk down the aisle that divided the two rows of stalls. "Horses again. It is becoming a theme with you. Perhaps after you become my mistress, if you are very good, I will buy one for you." He turned from the dark interior of the building and the muffled sounds of sleepy horses to walk over to one of two torches that were lit beside the entrance of the building. Their flames burned steadily, though they were giving off a great deal of thick gray smoke.

Lenobia watched him approach one of the torches. He stared at the flame with a look that was openly loving. His hand lifted and his fingers moved caressingly through the flame, causing the smoke to wave hazily around him. "That is what first drew me to you—the smoke of your eyes." He turned to look at her, the flame framing him. "But you knew that already. Women like you draw men to them on purpose, just as flame draws moths. You drew me and you drew that slave on the ship."

"I did not draw you," Lenobia said, refusing to speak to him of Martin.

"Ah, but obviously you did, because here I am." He spread out his arms. "And there is something I must make clear to you. I do not share what is mine. You are mine. I will not share you. So, little flame, do not draw any other moths to you, or I may have to snuff you, or them, out."

Lenobia shook her head and said the only thing she could think of: "You are absolutely mad. I am not yours. I will never be yours."

The priest frowned. "Well, then, I promise you that you will not belong to anyone else—not in this lifetime." He took a menacing step toward her, but black velvet swirled around him and it seemed a figure materialized out of smoke and night and shadow. The hood of the cloak fell back, and Lenobia gasped as the beautiful vampyre's face appeared. She smiled, lifted her hand, pointed a long finger at Lenobia, and said, "*Lenobia Whitehall! Night has chosen thee; thy death will be thy birth. Night calls to thee; hearken to Her sweet voice. Your destiny awaits you at the House of Night.*"

Pain exploded in Lenobia's forehead and she pressed both hands to her face. She wanted to sit there like that and believe that the entire night had been a nightmare—one long, unending, and terrifying dream—but the vampyre's next words had her lifting her head and blinking the bright spots free of her vision.

"Leave, Bishop. You have no hold on this daughter of Night. She now belongs to the Mother of all of us, the Goddess Nyx."

The Bishop's face was blazing as scarlet as the heavy cross that swayed from the chain around his neck. "You have ruined everything!" he shouted, blowing spittle at the vampyre.

"Begone, Darkness!" The vampyre didn't raise her voice, but it was filled with the power of her command. "I recognize you. Do not think you can hide from those who see you with more than human eyes. Begone!" As she repeated the command, the flames in the torches sputtered and almost extinguished completely.

The priest's red face paled and with one last, long look at Lenobia, he backed out of the stables and fled into the night.

Lenobia released the breath she had been holding in a gasp. "Is he gone? Truly?"

The vampyre smiled at her. "Truly. Neither he, nor any human, has authority over you now that Nyx has Marked you as her own."

Lenobia's hand lifted to the center of her forehead, which felt sore and bruised. "I am a vampyre?"

The Tracker laughed. "Not yet, daughter. Today you are a fledgling. Hopefully one day soon you will be a vampyre."

The sound of running footsteps had both of them turning defensively, but instead of the Bishop, it was Martin who burst into the stable. "*Cherie!* I followed the girls, but I stay back—so they don' see me—I don' know you leave them. Are you sick? Do you—" He broke off as what he was seeing seemed to register suddenly in his mind. He looked from Lenobia to the vampyre, and then quickly back to Lenobia, his gaze focused on the outline of the newly formed crescent in the middle of her forehead. "*Sacre bleu! Vampyre!*"

For an instant Lenobia's heart felt as if it would shatter, and she waited for Martin to reject her. He drew a deep breath and let it out with obvious relief. His smile began when he turned to the vampyre and bowed with a flourish, saying, "I am Martin. If what I believe to be true, true, I am the mate of Lenobia."

The vampyre's brows arched and her full lips tilted up in the hint of a smile. She fisted her right hand over her heart and said, "I am Medusa, Tracker for the Savannah House of Night. And though I see your intentions are honorable, you cannot officially be her mate until she is a fully Changed vampyre."

Martin bowed his head in acknowledgment. "Then I wait." When he turned his face toward Lenobia, the brilliance of his smile was the key to understanding, and the truth within her was freed.

"Martin and I—we can be together! We can be married?" Lenobia looked to Medusa.

The tall vampyre smiled. "At the House of Night, it is a woman's right to choose—mate or consort, black or white—what matters is choice." The vampyre included Martin in her smile. "And I see that you have made it. Though, perhaps as there is no House of Night in New Orleans, it would be best that Martin accompany you to Savannah."

"Is it possible? Really?" Lenobia said, her hands reaching for Martin as he moved to her side.

"It is," Medusa assured her. "And now that I see you have a true protector, I will allow the two of you time for yourselves. But do not tarry long. Return quickly to the dock and find the ship with the dragon as its masthead. I wait for you there, and we sail with the tide."

The vampyre must have left, but Lenobia saw only Martin and felt only his presence.

He took her hands in his. "What is it with horses and you, *cherie*? I find you with them again."

She couldn't stop smiling. "At least you will always know where to look for me."

"Good to know, *cherie,*" he said.

She slid her hands up his muscular chest until they rested on his broad shoulders. "Try not to lose me, you," she said, mimicking his accent.

"Never," he promised.

Then Martin bent and kissed her, and her entire world narrowed to only him. His taste imprinted on her senses, mixing indelibly with his scent and the wonderful feel of him that was thoroughly masculine, and uniquely Martin. He made a small, satisfied sound deep in his throat as her arms tightened around him. He deepened the kiss, and Lenobia lost herself in him, hardly knowing where her happiness ended and his began.

"Putain!"

Lenobia's joy was shattered by the sound of a curse. Martin reacted instantly. He whirled, pushing her behind him.

The Bishop had returned. He was standing at the entrance to the stables between the two torches. His arms were spread and the ruby cross at his breast was flashing in the flames that were growing taller and taller by the instant.

"Go now, you!" Martin said. "This girl, she don' choose you. She under my protection—sworn by vow—sealed by blood."

"No, you do not see. Her eyes make her mine. Her hair

makes her mine. But most of all, the power I carry makes her mine!" The Bishop reached his hands toward both torches. The flames leaped while smoke billowed, thickening until they licked his hands. Then, laughing horribly, he cupped the fire and threw it at the hay that was bundled into loose, dry bales all around them.

With a *whoosh!* the fire caught, fed, consumed. Lenobia knew a terrifying moment of heat and pain. She smelled her own hair burning. She opened her mouth to scream, but heat and smoke filled her lungs.

Then she felt his arms around her as Martin shielded her from the flames with his own body. He lifted her and carried her unflinchingly through the burning stable.

The warm, moist air in the street felt cold against Lenobia's singed skin when Martin staggered and lost his grip on her, and she fell to the street. She looked up at him. His body was burned so badly that all that was recognizable were his olive-and-amber eyes.

"Oh, no! Martin! No!"

"Too late, *cherie*. This world too late for us. I see you again, though. My love for you don' end here. My love for you, it never end."

She tried to stand, to reach for him, but her body was oddly weak, and movement had pain racing up her back.

"Die now, and leave *ma petite de bas* to me!" Behind Martin, the Bishop, silhouetted by the stable fire, began to move toward them.

Martin's gaze met hers. "I don' stay here now, though I wish I could. I don' lose you, either. I find you again, *cherie*. That I vow."

"Please, Martin. I do not want to live without you," she sobbed.

"You must. I find you again, *cherie*," he repeated. "Before I go, this one thing I can fix this time, though. *A bientôt, cher.* I will love you always."

Martin turned to meet the Bishop, who scoffed at him. "Still alive? Not for long!" Martin kept staggering toward the priest, speaking slowly and clearly:

> *"She belong to me—and hers I be!*
> *"Of loyalty and truth,*
> *"This blood be my proof!*
> *"What you do to her you do in vain.*
> *"What you cast come back on you tenfold the pain!"*

As he reached the Bishop, his movements changed. For just an instant he was swift and strong and whole again, but an instant was all Martin needed. His arms locked around Charles de Beaumont and, eerily mirroring the embrace that had saved Lenobia's life, Martin lifted the screaming, struggling Bishop and carried him into the burning inferno that had once been stables.

"Martin!" The shriek of agony that was wrenched from Lenobia was muffled by the awful sounds of panicked, burning horses and people rushing from nearby homes, shouting for water, shouting for help.

Through all the sounds and madness, Lenobia remained crumpled in the middle of the street, sobbing. As the flames spread and the world around her burned, she dropped her head and waited for the end.

"Lenobia! Lenobia Whitehall!"

She did not look up at the sound of her name. It was only the sound of a horse's nervous hooves on the cobblestones nearby that made her react. Medusa slid off the mare and knelt beside her. "Can you ride? We have little time. The city is burning."

"Leave me. I want to burn with it. I want to burn with him."

Medusa's eyes filled with tears. "Your Martin is dead?"

"And so am I," Lenobia said. "His death has killed me, too." As she spoke, Lenobia felt the depth of Martin's loss surge through her. It was too much—the pain was too much to contain within her body, and with a sob that was a widow's wail, she collapsed forward. The fabric along the back seam of her dress burst, and pain split her scorched skin.

"Daughter!" Medusa knelt beside her, reaching for her, trying to console her. "Your back—I must get you to the ship."

"Leave me here," Lenobia said again. "I vowed to never love another man, and I will not."

"Keep your vow, daughter, but live. Live the life he could not."

Lenobia began to refuse, and then the soft muzzle of the mare dropped to her, blew against her singed hair, and nuzzled her face.

And through her pain and despair, Lenobia felt it—felt the mare's worry, as well as her fear at the spreading fire.

"I can feel what she does." Lenobia reached a weak, trembling hand up to stroke the horse. "She is worried and afraid."

"It is your gift—your affinity. They rarely manifest this soon. Listen to me, Lenobia. Our Goddess, Nyx, has given you this great gift. Do not reject it and the comfort and, perhaps, happiness it could bring to you."

Horses and happiness . . .

The second story of the house beside the stables collapsed, and sparks cascaded around them, setting fire to the silk curtains in the house across the street.

The mare's fear spiked—and it was the horse's terror that made Lenobia move. "I can ride," she said, allowing Medusa to help her to her feet and then lift her into the saddle.

Medusa gaped. "Your back! It—it is bad. This will be painful, but once we are aboard the ship I can help you to heal, though you will always bear the scars of this night."

The vampyre mounted the mare, pointed her toward the docks, and gave her her head. As they galloped to safety and the mystery of a new life, Lenobia closed her eyes and repeated to herself:

I will love you until the day I die—only you, Martin. Always only you; I vow it.